STEPBROTHER, PLEASE STOP TEASING ME!

Volume Fourteen

MIA CLARK

Cherrylily

This is a work of fiction. Similarities to real people, places, or events are
entirely coincidental.

Stepbrother, Please Stop Teasing Me!
(Volume Fourteen)

Copyright © 2023 Mia Clark

Written by Mia Clark

All rights reserved.

CONTENTS

ABOUT THE BOOK

Shy good girl Charlotte Scott secretly writes steamy romance stories in the library after school.

And after a lot of difficulty with the hot and heavy scenes, she's almost finished writing her first book!

She would like to give a special thank you to her new stepbrother, Hunter Jackson, who has always been there to:

- A.) Tease her relentlessly
- B.) Let her give him a nice lap dance even though she wasn't sure what she was doing at first
- C.) Pretend to be her husband so they can get a free weekend getaway in Las Vegas
- D.) All of the above

(P.S. ~ It's D.)

Now that she's looking at the end of her first steamy romance novel, things are looking up and Charlotte's ready for a well-deserved break.

...If she can actually pull off pretending to be someone else for the weekend, that is.

And, to make matters worse, it's the first time in a long time she's been all alone with Hunter, and, um...

They can do whatever they want all weekend?
She has ideas.
So many ideas.
All the ideas.
(Full steam ahead?!)

THE FUN HAS JUST BEGUN...

Episode 175

CHARLOTTE

"Now let's pick our winner!" Bella shouts to the club full of people. "Unfortunately we had a couple girls who needed to leave and two who had a little too much fun and broke the rules," she adds, playfully pouting as if this happens all the time. "Don't worry, though! We still have plenty of lovely ladies left and I'm sure we can choose one to take it all, right?"

Everyone claps. Um, Clarissa and Angela clap, too. None of the rest of the girls sitting in the special reserved section clap so I don't know if we're supposed to clap but also the cheerleaders aren't in the competition anymore so maybe that's fine?

I'm really confused and the only saving grace is that I'm wearing my own sneakers again. My feet feel a lot more steady and comfortable.

"Can the girls that are still in the competition head up on stage please? Just line up and spread out in a circle. We're going to have a round of applause for each and every one of these ladies so we can show them how amazing they are.

But... and this is important! The girl with the *loudest* applause is going to be declared our amateur night winner. I expect cheering for every single one of them, but make sure you make it *loud* for the girl you want to win. Got it?"

That's, um... that's me. Us. We're the girls. It's... oh gosh...

Jenny and Hannah start to stand and they look really nervous too so that makes me feel slightly better, at least. The other two women who came together also stand with us. I hurry after them and try to hide in the back but Jenny and Hannah grab one of my hands each and squeeze it tight. We go up together, all three of us, and the two other women flash us big friendly smiles as soon as we step on the stage right after they do.

"We'll do this in order of performance," Bella declares, belting out the words instead of using her microphone. "Can I hear a round of applause for *Cherry Delight!*"

Jenny hops forward quick and takes a bow as the crowd cheers for her. She also scans the audience quick, eyes landing on Teddy, who looks unsure if he should cheer or not?

"Teddy!" Jenny whispers loudly at him. "What are you doing!"

"I didn't even see you dance!" Teddy loudly whispers back. I think they're trying to be quiet but everyone can hear them?

"So?!"

"It wouldn't be fair if I cheered for you, Jenny," he protests.

"That's not the point! You're supposed to cheer anyways!"

Reluctantly, Teddy starts to clap except the time for clapping is over now so it's just, um... it's only two quick claps?

Jenny huffs and glares at her brother as she heads back to the lineup and Bella carries on with the show.

The two other women step up next, one after the other. They clap for each other and I think that's really nice so I clap for them, too.

And then...

"Now let's hear it for *Roxy!*" Bella yells to the crowd, who is more than happy to cheer for one of their favorites.

Hannah was really good, too. Olly cheers the loudest, which I think makes her blush even if she's trying to hide it. She glances quickly at him and then looks away, her cheeks at least three shades redder after. She grins and smiles and I cheer for her too and so does Amelia and since Amelia's cheering so does Sam, and Teddy claps for Hannah even though Jenny's glaring hard at him for it and, um...

"And finally..." Bella says, slowly leading up to it. I know what's next but I got distracted clapping for Hannah so I'm not even remotely ready. "The sexy and oh-so-talented *Chantel!*"

...I don't know if I'm sexy or talented even if I liked my dance except Bella's much better and I'm sure all the strippers who work here are really really good, so...

I stumble to the front of the stage and I expect a little bit of clapping, mainly from Hunter, but it's way more than I thought?

Like, um... not just from Hunter but from everyone else, too?

Chloe cheers me on like I'm a masterpiece and she's admiring fine art. The cheerleaders clap and cheer and whistle and shout, "Go Chantel! Love you, babe!" Teddy claps and smiles wide and so does Sam and Olly does too but I think he's trying to cheer just a little bit less for me than he did for Hannah. That's okay, though. Thank you still, Olly. I... I appreciate it! I, um...

Jenny and Hannah are cheering for me too and that's confusing because we're supposed to be competing against each other but I don't know if I'm very good at that and I cheered for them also, so, um...

The other women on stage who I don't even know that well are clapping for me, too.

3

"You really were amazing!" one of them says, hushed, for me and me alone.

"I wish I could do what you did," the other adds, excited.

This goes on and on for a long long time and I'm getting more nervous and embarrassed by the second and I kind of want to, um... I'm going to wake up and this'll all be a dream but thankfully it'll be fine because it'll be a dream I had while sleeping in bed with Hunter and I can shyly tell him about it and he'll laugh and then we'll, um... do fun things that don't involve clothes and fall asleep again and I won't remember any of this in the morning, and...

Um, nope. This is not a dream.

"I'd say we have a clear winner then," Bella says. "Ladies and gentleman, Chantel! We'll get you your prize in a second, beautiful. And that's the end of amateur night, but it's definitely not the end of tonight. Don't forget, we'll have our usual roundup of girls performing for you on stage after this and all the ladies of amateur night are welcome to use the private rooms at their discretion. Gentlemen! Ladies, too! Feel free to *ask*, but no means no. Girls, if you feel uncomfortable at any point, let one of us know and we'll handle it. We want you to have fun and feel safe. And so... Crystal, hit us with a song to end things off!"

"Got it!" Crystal calls back, immediately pressing play on, um...

I don't know who sings it but it's that song about pouring sugar on someone?

"Did you *seriously* have to pick the most cliche stripper song in history?" Bella snaps, glaring at her.

"It's a classic!" Crystal replies, laughing. "Everyone loves it but you."

"Everyone but me needs to get a new favorite stripclub song."

Crystal cackles and pokes her tongue out at Bella, who just rolls her eyes and shakes her head.

And, um... amateur night is over? Kind of. The contest is over, but...

Can I bring Hunter into a private room now? Wait, is it alright if I ask him or do I need to wait for him to ask me?

HUNTER

Amateur night's finished, but I feel like tonight's only just begun.

Except also, fuck, it's a Thursday and we have class tomorrow so it's not like we can stay until the place shuts down, so, uh... just fuck. That's it.

To be fair, I don't want to close the place down, either. Mainly I want to get my hot ass fucking stepsister somewhere private so I can finally do what I've wanted to since I first saw her in her outfit for the night. Which, you know, was apparently just the tip of the iceberg and holy fucking shit the trick she pulled on the pole where she intentionally ripped her clothes or whatever to reveal that nice and naughty set of lingerie underneath...

I'm hard as hell and I don't have a lot more to say about that except I want to put it to good use as soon as possible.

"So, um... did I win the triathlon event, though?" Baby Sis asks when we're all sitting together after Bella handed out the prize money and had a final chat with the other girls. "I don't know how that works?"

"I mean, you won the amateur night contest, right?" I say with a shrug. "I'd say yes"

"You *totally* won, babe!" Angela says, steadfast and supportive. "Also, oh my gosh, *how?* Charlie! Where've you been hiding those hot moves, babe?!"

"Umm... Jenny and I... we g-go to classes and..." she mumbles, picking at her nails, staring at her fingertips. "And, um... that's it."

The two other women who didn't get kicked out of the

contest hurry over before anyone can say much more. They gush and giggle and quickly introduce themselves to Baby Sis and the girls.

"I'm Mary," one says. The other adds right after, "I'm Nina!"

"You girls were so good," Mary tells them. "Do you go to classes? We'd love to check them out sometime if you don't mind sharing where you go?"

"Yes, please," Nina says, nodding, grinning ear to ear. "This has always been a bucket list thing for us and we used to go to pole dancing classes years ago when we were still in college, but you girls inspired us to pick it up again."

"You were *amazing*, by the way," Mary adds, reaching over the table to rest her fingers on my stepsister's arm. "I mean, wow. I would've thought you did this for a living."

"Um, no," Baby Sis says, shaking her head super fast. "...Thank you, though!"

"Charlie's so cool," Clarissa agrees. "We love her. I want to go to classes, too. I mean, we kind of have to, right? Like, well, technically *you* do, Angela. You got dared by Teddy during Truth or Dare night. I want to go so bad now, though! *Ple~ase!*"

"Everyone can go," Jenny says, hands crossed over her chest, looking slightly peeved about something. Probably Teddy. Poor dude. "We take classes with Rhonda. Um, me, Charlotte, and Hannah do. It's just Pole Dancing with Rhonda if you look it up online. She's really good."

"She *is* good, but I don't even know where Charlotte got all her moves from because I don't remember learning those in class?" Hannah adds. "It's an exercise class first and foremost, and it's really fun, but..."

"I... I watched a lot of YouTube pole dancing tutorials..." Baby Sis mumbles. "And, um... I asked Rhonda if I had any questions and she showed me the moves in person and... that's it, really. She was really nice and helpful."

"We'll totally check the classes out," Mary says. "Hopefully we'll see you there."

"Yes, definitely," Nina adds, smiling and waving to the girls.

I feel like the dude's in this place are an afterthought and all the girls just want to talk about pole dancing and how cute everyone is and... I'm kind of into it, actually? Baby Sis looks like she's having a blast and she keeps smiling and giggling and getting excited over the most random things I never would've thought were exciting, but to her they are.

It's stupidly fucking hot seeing her like this right now and my hard-on is only getting harder. Goddamn, buddy. Calm down.

My dick doesn't listen to a word I say. Oh well.

Also as to whether Baby Sis won tonight's event for my ex-girlfriend's dumbass Stepbro Triathlon--

Her phone buzzes and she jumps, startled, pulling it out and checking it fast. She's sitting right next to me and angles it so I can see and read the screen, too. The text is from Erica, which she added as a contact into her phone at some point, but also on top of my ex's name she tossed in an angry face emoji at the end which seems fitting.

ERICA (WHY IS SHE SO MEAN?)

"Chantelotte or whatever the heck your real name is. Yes, alright, I admit defeat for this event, but that doesn't mean you've won. You may be thinking, but, Erica, that's two out of three Stepbro Triathlon events I've won and clearly that means I'm the ultimate winner. You're WRONG, though. Super duper freaking 100% wrong! Because the last event is worth a hundred points and the winner of that one gets Huntsy as their one true stepbro, to have and to hold and to do as many dirty freaky things as possible with. Like, if he's there with you, tell him I'm going to sneak those blue erection pills into his breakfast every morning so he'll be hard and thinking about me all the time and he'll just have to take out his frustrations on my wet slippery little... well, you get the idea."

"Anywho! You may think you're great or whatever but you're not and the next and final event is winner takes all. I'll clearly be the winner this time. It's a written exam about our stepbros and you probably don't even know anything about Huntsy or what he likes or what his actual purpose as a stepbro is so, like, just give up, 'kay? TTYL. Oh and if Lance is still there, tell him I'm going to wear the same outfit I wore to the club to bed so if he liked it he can see it again up close and personally by sneaking into my room at midnight and, like, finally doing his duty as my stepbro for once in his life. Ugh, what an idiot. I don't even understand."

"...So does she like Lance or not?" Baby Sis asks me, trying to read between the squiggliest fucking lines known to man. Like, there's not even any lines to read between here. Erica's fucked up in the head. That's all. That's it.

"I think she's just weird as hell and kind of mean?" I answer. "Probably don't think about it too much."

"Okay," Baby Sis says, nodding, as if this is a perfectly acceptable answer. I mean, it is, but I didn't think she'd accept it so quickly, you know?

"Anyways, *Charlie!*" Clarissa says, giddy, somehow hopping up and down in her seat. It's like a bounce bounce bounce thing and she's still wearing her latex tube top and I swear she's going to fall out of that shit real soon. "You won! Totally! Yay!"

"Yay," Baby Sis says, clapping her hands together. "That was so fun, right?"

"So fun, babe!" Angela agrees. "But, like, can I change into my regular clothes now? The boob sweat is real with this top. Latex, am I right?"

"It really is," Clarissa says with a nod. "Also guys keep asking us to give them lap dances?"

"I mean, that's kind of flattering, though?"

"Like... maybe? But how do you give a lap dance?" Clarissa asks, oddly wholesome sounding. "I totally know how to cheer and dance and do the splits and cartwheels and somersaults and flips and, like... but how do you do that in someone's lap?"

"You're asking how to cheer while sitting in a dude's lap?" Olly asks, suddenly finding this conversation relevant to his interests.

"Um, yes?"

"I could show you, I guess," he says with a shrug. "If you need help."

...I don't think this is the kind and benevolent offer Clarissa thinks it is, especially with the way Olly's flashing his teeth in a mischievous smirk...

"Really, could you?! That's so nice!"

"No!" Jenny snaps, shutting that shit down real fast. "Shut up, Olly! Not happening!"

"I mean, I could use some help with it, too?" Angela says, turning her lusty gaze towards my boy, Teddy. "Um, if you're not too busy maybe, Teddy?"

"Huh?" Teddy says, blinking. "It's not that I'm busy or anything, but it's a lap dance, right?" he points out. "I don't think it's supposed to involve cheer-style dancing. It's more like, you know... it's just different?"

"What *is* it exactly, buddy?" Sam says, goading him on. "You're the one with experience now. What happened when you went into a private room with not just one, but two attractive women?"

"Dude, that was completely different," Teddy says, defensive. "I was trying to help! Anyways, nothing really happened? It was just, like... some dancing?"

"In your lap?"

"I guess so, yeah?"

"Can we please not talk about my brother getting a lap dance," Jenny pipes in. "Thanks!"

"Right," I say, trying to pull this conversation back to what's important. Or, you know, what I think's important. Fuck. "Speaking of lap dances..."

I'm doing my best to insinuate to Baby Sis that we should take our leave for however long it takes to enjoy a little private time together in one of the lap dance rooms, except she doesn't get it, not even close. I nod at her and she... nods back... blinking a whole lot, brow scrunched up tight, staring at me in between the blinking.

"Ohhh!" she finally says.

Yes. There we go. You got this, Baby Sis.

...She does not, in fact, have it...

CHARLOTTE

I didn't *forget* forget, but I, um... I kind of forgot? The romance book club girls are here and they're reading a short romance novella about a girl who finds love in a stripclub and that's what Hunter means, right? Right.

So, you know... I take his hand and we excuse ourselves from our one group of friends and head over to our other group of friends and, um...

Hunter looks incredibly forlorn as soon as we sit down but I'm sure it's just because he wishes we'd read the story earlier since we're behind in the discussion now.

Also Ruby's sitting here too and she's apparently really into this story.

"I mean, there's always the fantasy, right?" she says to the book club girls. "I totally get it, girls. But trust me, the reality doesn't live up to the ideas in this book or the ideas you might have about what happens. Mostly, when you work in a stripclub you get a handful of regulars, which are super nice and respectful but they tend to be the older men who either don't get a lot of attention at home or were never married to begin with or maybe have gone through a divorce. Those are the bill payers, and they aren't always the hottest guys ever, but they're so appreciative and they look at you in the nicest way and you can't help but enjoy your time with them, right?"

"Is that like the older silver fox billionaire type then?" Holly asks, hopeful.

"Some have money, and some are cute enough in that older man kind of way, but I don't know if I'd go so far as to say they're silver fox billionaires, no."

"Clearly the story took some liberties," Joanna says, grinning. "It's nice to know what's real and what isn't, though."

"What about, like... the younger guys, though?" Amanda asks. "Oh oh oh! What about the second chance romance angle? Like the boy you had a crush on in highschool but he was shy and introverted and only really came into his own after college when he bulked up and got even hotter. And he shows up at the stripclub as part of his friend's bachelor party and you see him and he sees you and even though it starts out as a lost connection catching up thing, once you show him your moves in a private room things take a turn for the stupidly hot and sexy and--"

"Whoa whoa whoa, calm your hormones over there, girl!" Ruby says, giggling. "Okay, first off, bachelor parties? The *worst*. I'm not even joking. You make a lot of money, but sometimes it's not worth the hassle. A lot of times it's just this soon-to-be married guy's friends trying to 'talk to you in private' and offering to pay extra to show the groom one last night of hot stripper ecstasy before he's tied down forever to the poor girl he's about to marry. It's really weird. And if it's not that, the guys treat you like an object and act as if throwing money at you means you need to do whatever they want. The only time I've had fun with a bachelor party was when the bride came too and she was into it and we gave *her* a lap dance in front of her man. Now *that's* fun."

"Unless," Bella says, coming over to interrupt. "The bride also has a stripper fetish and tries to get too handsy. Not as fun. Trust me. Been there, done that."

"You tell that story all the time and I really think you're bragging about it now because that's never happened to me," Ruby says, rolling her eyes and sticking her tongue out at her work friend.

"What can I say, I'm just that hot," Bella says, tossing her platinum blonde hair over her shoulder, puffing up her chest, and lifting her chin.

"Shut up. We know, bitch."

"Do you have, um... like... boyfriend trouble, though?" I ask. I want to read the story but I haven't yet but I also want to ask questions so...

"Yeah, that's hard," Ruby admits. "I mean, a lot of girls end up with jealous boyfriend problems. Or, and we're not supposed to do this, but sometimes you think a guy you meet in here is cool so you agree to spend time with him outside the club, and he thinks that means you're into him more than you are and he shows up more often and then he wants to take over your time when you're working and he wants a bunch of freebies and... yup, no thanks. This is my job. I need to work when I'm here, you know?"

"Just don't date," Bella says, matter-of-fact. "Problem solved."

"Easy for you to say, Bella!" Ruby snaps back. "Some of us have basic needs that need dealing with."

"All my basic needs can be solved by a pack of batteries and an impulse purchase from the Lola website. Learn how to pleasure yourself and you'll never need a man again."

Ruby sighs. "As if it's that easy."

"Anyways, I didn't come here to chat about your high libido issues," Bella says. "Charlotte. Or Chantel? Which do you prefer now, hun?"

"Um, can I be Chantel still?" I ask.

"You can be whoever you want to be," Bella says, winking at me.

I giggle and smile and she smirks and laughs back.

"My set's up soon if you want to see what I do in the club? I know you were curious at Saskia's shop but that was only a quick show. Bring your boy if you want. You two are welcome to sit at my stage while I perform. I told the guys to leave you alone so don't worry about putting money up. Let my usual gentleman do that, alright?"

...I really want to see Bella dance...

But, um... is it weird if I ask Hunter to sit with me?

"Is, um... is that okay?" I ask him.

"Am I supposed to get upset that you want to sit and watch a stripper strip?" he counters.

"Um, maybe?"

"I don't get fully naked," Bella says, straight-faced. "The

bra comes off, though. Need to keep my adoring fans entertained."

"All in the name of Bella's adoring fans..." Ruby says, rolling her eyes. "And money."

"It's not my fault if they think I'm worth it," Bella says, smirking. "You have your own fans, you know?"

"They only like the cheerleader routines, though!" Ruby huffs. "I'm not even a cheerleader anymore! I graduated two years ago!"

"You're just so good at it, baby girl..." Bella purrs.

"Stop that or I'll start getting ideas."

Bella winks back. "I'll bring the toys and the batteries..."

Oh gosh. What.

And, um...

"Just gonna head to the bathroom quick," Hunter says, fidgeting in place. "Be right back."

"Okay," I say to him, nodding.

Bella glances between me and Hunter with a look that, um... I think she sees something but I don't know what it is because I don't see it?

"Poor baby..." Bella says to Hunter.

Oh no. Is he not feeling well? Is he sick? We can leave! If, um... I hope we can stay until after Bella dances but if Hunter's not feeling good then that's more important and we can go back to the dorms and...

He shrugs it off and heads to the bathroom and the romance book club girls show me the stripper romance story on their phones and I start to read it while waiting for Bella's set to start and--

It takes me a lot longer than I think it should to realize Hunter has a very strong erection. I'm literally the last to know. But, um, when I *do* figure it out?

That's coming soon and it's a lot of fun...

BELLA'S BEST ADVICE

Episode 176

HUNTER

Holy fuck, I'm trying my best here but I'm about to fucking lose it.

I've been half-hard since I first saw my stepsister in her silk robe, a hint of the outfit she was wearing underneath peeking through. Little did I know there was so much more to it, though.

And, uh, yeah... I've been harder than hard since I saw her up on stage during the amateur night competition. It's becoming an issue.

Look, clearly I'm not about to jerk off in the stripclub bathroom. First, because that's weird as hell. Second, because I'm saving this particular erection for later.

But...

Even if I *did* do that, I'm pretty fucking sure I'd be hard again as soon as I stepped out of here. The memories of Baby Sis in her hot as hell lacy pink and black bra and panties, moving on the pole like she fucking owns it... yeah, imprinted in my brain forever.

This is my life now. I'm going to be perpetually erect and it's all my stepsister's fault.

I guess there's worse problems to have?

Anyways, I actually use the bathroom and then I head back out to check in with the boys, and, uh...

"Where'd the girls go?" I ask, because they're gone. Completely fucking vanished.

"Can I be real with you for a second?" Olly says, a moment of unusual gravity.

"Is it about strippers?" I ask him. "If so, no."

"Usually I'd agree with you, Jacksy," Sam counters. "But we're in a stripclub. It's more relevant now than it's ever been."

"There's actually not much else to talk about besides strippers here, is there?" Teddy points out, apparently agreeing with Sam and Olly.

"I don't want to ruin this for you guys, but nobody ever *has* to talk about strippers, you know?"

"I'm not saying we *have* to," Olly says. "I'm not even saying we *should*. What I was going to say is... I feel like the girls love the strippers more than we do? Like, come on, I thought I'd be completely fucking hyped to be here tonight, and, don't get me wrong, it's fun. Everywhere you look, there's hot, half-naked women of literally every kind of beauty imaginable. There's the big-chested ladies. The lithe athletic girls. There's women with seriously impressive asses and not as much up top. Or ones in the middle with a little bit of everything. And that's great. I won't ever complain. But for real, the girls are way more excited about this and I feel like we've failed somehow, you know?"

"What did we fail at?" Teddy asks. "I thought we came here to support the girls?"

"We did, Teddy," I say. "We really did. But Olly has a point. I've been thinking it, too."

"It's not that I haven't been thinking it," Sam adds. "But do you think it's too much if I ask Amelia if she wants to get a lap dance from Crystal?"

"Dude, why Crystal? She's kind of a bitch, isn't she?"

"I know she was giving Bella shit during the contest but Chloe and Amelia keep going to watch her dance and I want to take my ego out of the picture and focus on what Amelia would be into, you know?"

"Just because they're watching Crystal dance on stage doesn't mean they're into her, dude," I point out. "It's a stripclub. There's not much else to do."

"Sure, but Crystal asked Amelia if she wanted to see a cool trick and basically she did a headstand while Amelia leaned forward and completely squished her tits in her face, so..."

"Seriously," I say, unsure if I should be offended or not. "The girls like the stripclub way more than us."

"I don't even know where Hannah is anymore," Olly adds. "Do I give up now or what?"

"Oh, they all went to watch Bella dance," Teddy says, nodding towards the far end of the showroom. "Hannah and Jenny got excited because Baby Charlie told them how good Bella is and then Clarissa and Angela wanted to watch too, and--" He pauses and blinks at us as we all stare at him. "Why are you guys looking at me like that?"

"How do you always know where the girls are?" Olly asks him. "Seriously."

"I don't know why you don't," Teddy says with a shrug. "It's kind of obvious, isn't it?"

"Uh, no," I tell him. "It's not."

"Bella *is* really good, by the way," Teddy says, getting right back to it. "She showed me some of her signature moves when she was trying to help Angela and... wow. I mean, I'm not a stripclub connoisseur but I was seriously impressed. It's like you just know when you see her dance that it's good, you know?"

"Fuck off, Teddy," Olly snaps.

"Agreed," I say, rolling my eyes.

"What?" Teddy says, confused. "What'd I do?"

"Guys, be nice to Teddy. Just because he's an oblivious sex magnet, that doesn't mean we should hate on him. We should learn from him and do our best to support our bud."

"Thanks, Sam," Teddy says, appreciative. "I don't know what you mean by sex magnet, though. I was just helping."

"Look, this was great," I tell them. "Nice talk or whatever. But I'm going to go find my amateur night winning girlfriend now. Don't wait for me, boys."

"Say hi to Baby Charlie for me!" Teddy says. "Uh, can you ask Jenny if Ruby can show me another song, too? She was asking but I didn't want Jenny to get mad. I don't know why she would, but she's being weird tonight, so..."

"Fuck *off*, Teddy!" Olly grunts. "Holy fucking shit!"

"What the hell, Olly?" Teddy counters. "I can ask her to share the song with you too if you want?"

"No. I refuse. I'm not accepting a pity lap dance from your new hot stripper friend."

"I'm sure she'd be fine with it. I mean, she does it for a living and as long as you're nice and can pay her it's alright?"

"I said what I said and I'm sticking to it."

"Is this because of Hannah?" Sam asks. "If so, wow. You're really into her, huh?"

"Ohhhhhh, is *that* why Olly's being weird tonight?" Teddy asks.

I don't hear much more because I'm too far away and the music's blasting, or starting to, and...

There she is:

Bella climbs on stage in her work outfit, which, uh... you know, she's a stripper so there's not much to it. That's great, super cool, whatever. She's attractive, alright? I get it.

Anyways, the thing that draws my attention is the way Baby Sis is sitting alongside the stage, hands clasped in her lap, staring up at Bella with awe and admiration, a look of pure shimmering wonder in her eyes.

I think my girlfriend accidentally fell in love with a stripper, man. Fuck.

I mean, it's like a platonic friendship kind of love, so it's cool, but still.

I honestly never thought Baby Sis would come out of her shell even more at a stripclub of all places, but here we are, and...

"Gentleman," Bella says to the men sitting on the other side of the stage from the girls. "The girls are here as my guests, alright? I'm going to put on my best show, but since there's less space at the stage, could you do me the favor of tipping a little extra for them? It would really make me happy. I mean, look at them? So cute, aren't they? This song is for my new friend, Chantel. I knew you could do it, baby. I'm so proud of you. I hope your boy knows how lucky he is."

I do. I am. Fuck, do I know it.

...I still want to drag my stepsister's sexy ass into a private room for a lap dance as soon as humanly possible, but...

I'm really proud of her, too.

CHARLOTTE

I watch, entranced, as Bella does a really amazing dance to this song, um...

It's *W.I.T.C.H.* by Devon Cole except she's using the Rain Paris remix version which is a little more rock and less pop? (At least that's what I'm told afterwards when I ask about it but as I watch it I just kind of listen and pay attention and see what she does and how everyone reacts and...)

I also don't fully get the witch part at first because instead of that it just says she's a *Woman In Total Control of Herself,* which is super fun and empowering and I really love *that* idea too and--

S-sorry! I'm just really excited right now.

Bella moves and sways on the pole, sliding across the stage, showing her body off for the men on the other side, doing difficult pole work for me and the girls on this side. It's like she's in a trance, knowing exactly what to do when she needs to do it but none of it looks like she's performing, per se. It's so fluid and seamless and amazing. I don't think I could ever do anything like that.

And then, um... I mean, about halfway through once she's decided her adoring gentlemen have put enough money on the stage she reaches back, unclips her shiny black bra, letting it fall to the floor as she climbs the pole as if it's a witch's broom and, um...

She does a wild falcon, which I'm pretty sure is to show off for both us and the men because it's really hard to do and also it's, um... one leg hooked high up on the pole while the other does a kind of split, sliding downwards, and you lean backwards, back arched towards the floor, spinning slightly exactly like that, basically showing off your chest. Which Bella does, to the wide-eyed excitement of her gentleman fans.

Bella transitions into a reverse moon after that, holding the pole higher up with both hands, the metal rod nestled between her thighs, back arched upwards this time, chest pushed out. It looks like a crescent moon kind of, so, you know... the name, um, *reverse moon,* and...

She finishes with some groundwork, looking absolutely magical and witchy and super sexy and really pretty and I hope these men won't miss their money because they put a lot of it on stage for her at this point and, um, wow...

The song ends and Bella winks at one man in particular, who I think probably comes here often and she's going to spend time with later. She leans in close and whispers something to him. He nods and steps away from the stage for now, heading back to a table he reserved earlier.

"Oh my God," Jenny says to us as Bella makes her way over to our side of the stage. "Guys, for real. What the heck just happened? That was amazing!"

"I know, right!" I squeak, excited. "The wild falcon is really hard to do."

"Like, I have no idea what that is, but does anyone else wish they had a body like that?" Angela asks. "I've totally never felt insecure before, and, like... I don't know if I feel insecure now, but, *totally*, you know?"

"*Totally*..." Clarissa says, wistful. "I completely know what you mean."

"I'd settle for the boobs," Hannah says. "And the moves. Is that a thing? Boobs and moves? I feel like I'm onto something here."

"Girls, go away," Bella says, glaring at us. "It's time for you to dote on your boys. Which one belongs to who?"

"Um, Hunter is mine," I say, lifting my hand to answer the question as if we're in class.

Bella stares at me, slowly blinking, one dark brow raised. "I know that already, honey."

"Oh."

"Teddy's my brother?" Jenny offers. "Does that count?"

"Real or step?" Bella asks.

"Real."

"No, it doesn't. Try again."

"Can, um... like, I don't know if he's *mine*," Hannah says slowly. "But I *did* tell Olly I'd play *Spellcraft: The Scattering* with him later, so..."

"Go," Bella says. "Claim your man before someone else does. Trust me, any of the girls working tonight will gladly do it for you if you don't."

"Yes, ma'am!" Hannah says, hopping out of her chair, ready to run.

"Don't run," Bella snaps. "*Never* run after a man. Always walk. Be like a cat. Look entirely uninterested, stretch your body a little, don't look him in the eyes while you're heading over, pretend you're not even going near him, and then when he least expects it you curl into his lap and take what you want."

"...That's totally the most amazing advice I've ever heard in my entire life," Clarissa says, dumbstruck. "Wow..."

Hannah nods, reverent, and attempts to be a cat now. I think she can do it. She kind of has a cat-like look already? I don't know why I think that but I just think it, so, um... yes?

"So, like, I'm going to see if Teddy's okay, you know?" Angela says, shifty-eyed. "Not for any particular reason! He's just, like, a little clueless sometimes, am I right? I'll protect him from the strippers for you, Jenny. Don't even worry, babe!"

Bella stares at Angela, shaking her head. Jenny doesn't notice, though.

"Yeah, he really is oblivious, isn't he?" Jenny says with a sigh. "Ugh. Thanks, Angela. Teddy just doesn't understand and I try to tell him and it's like... ugh!"

"Okay, that's three down," Bella says. "Who's next?"

"Sam's with Amelia," I point out. "I think that's all the boys?"

"Jenny! You want to be my pretend man tonight?" Clarissa asks. "I'll, like, totally tell you how pretty you are and we can talk about clothes."

"Heck yeah!" Jenny says, giggling. "Sounds fun. Do I have to buy you a drink or are you buying me one?"

"What if we totally buy each other drinks?"

"Cool. Sounds good."

"Weird but sure, go have fun," Bella tells them. "Shoo shoo. I have to talk to this one now."

Right, so, um... that's me, apparently. Me and Bella, sitting by the stage, which at first isn't too strange except it's another girl's set and she's already dancing. Bella rolls her eyes at me and tells me to ignore it but it's kind of hard because she has a really impressive butt and she apparently knows exactly how to shake it for maximum male attention and financial gain.

...I didn't know this was a thing before but the dollar bills on stage speak for themselves...

"So what's next, my beautiful little butterfly?" Bella asks me. "What are your plans for the rest of the night?"

"Ummmm..." I mumble, shy. "I... I w-want to give Hunter a lap dance but I don't know how?"

"It's a lap, honey. You dance in it. There's not much more to it."

"...Yes," I say, quietly nodding. "But do I ask *him* or do I wait for him to ask *me*? I've never given a lap dance before?"

"Here's a quick piece of advice," Bella says, patting me on the shoulder. "You learn this real quick when you start working in the club. You *never* want a man to approach you for a lap dance. The kind of man who approaches you is always going to be a huge unknown. He's coming to you because he likes how you look, pure and simple. There's nothing more to it than that. You might think that's good in this industry, but trust me, it's not. You want to go to the man first, chat him up, see what he's like, how he talks to you, if he's going to respect you and your boundaries, and then and only then do you invite him to the back for a lap dance. But *only* if you're feeling it, understand? If there's *anything* that sets you off. Anything. Any small, little, inconsequential thing whatsoever, you stop immediately, make an excuse to leave, and go find someone else to try out. Trust your instincts. They'll never steer you wrong."

"Okay," I say with a nod. "Wait, um... so if Hunter asks me first then I shouldn't give him a lap dance? But if I ask him first it's fine?"

"I mean, your case is different, but I'd stick to the advice if I were you. If he asks you first he's *really* desperate and that sounds fun, don't you think? Make him squirm and toy with him first. And if you ask him first, you're in control, so... make him squirm and toy with him first. Either way works."

...She makes it sound so easy and it sounds really fun, but... I don't know if I can actually do it?

"I know you can do it, baby," she says, smirking. "Do you know how I know?"

"How?" I ask.

I think she's going to say something about how she sees something in me that, um... I don't actually know what, but it reminds her of me or the way I was able to dance tonight or maybe because she recognizes a long lost ex that she wished she'd stayed with in Hunter and she doesn't want me to have the same regrets she does or...

She doesn't say any of this and after she answers I feel kind of dumb.

"He was watching the stage the entire time I was up there but instead of staring at my tits he was watching you watch me instead. He's all yours already. Enjoy him."

I, um... I blink and when Bella covertly nods behind me I turn to look and...

Hunter's there, pretending not to look at me but he definitely is and I can see it and our eyes lock together for a fraction of a second before he looks away, pretending not to look at me again. I keep watching him just in case and then he looks back again and...

"Okay, do it fast before he asks you because I need to put you both out of your misery," she says, snickering. "You two want it so bad it's starting to hurt me just watching you."

Bella starts to get up, to leave, to go spend time with the man who is apparently going to pay her a lot of money for conversation, flirting, and, um... probably lap dances but I don't really know.

Anyways--

"W-wait!" I mumble. "Um, how do I give a lap dance, though? Do you have any tips? Please!"

"Tips, eh?" Bella says, considering it. "I *do* have one, but... you have to be strict about it. Understand? Tell him this as soon as you get back there and he'll be yours forever, but you can't break this rule while you're in the back no matter what."

"Wait, forever, really?!" I ask, a little too excited.

"Calm down," Bella says, giggling. "That might've been an exaggeration, but... yes."

I nod and listen and she tells me and--

It's very simple advice but also somehow amazing? I... I don't know if, um...

"Just when you're out back," Bella adds, grinning at me. "Once you're home, anything goes."

I nod. I can do this. Stay strong, Charlotte. It's for the greater good. It's for Hunter. It's, um...

Will he really be mine *forever* though?

...Oh gosh...

HUNTER

I'm trying my hardest to let Baby Sis have fun with her friends instead of dragging her off to have some fun because seriously I have the strongest erection of my entire fucking life right now and it's pretty much all her fault.

I mean that in the nicest way possible. Seriously, feel free to make my cock as hard as you want anytime you want, Baby Sis. It's yours for the taking.

Anyways, yeah... I take my eye off her for a second because she's chatting it up with Bella about stripper stuff or who knows what and then suddenly she's sitting next to me, curling up close, her hands wrapped around my arm as she stares into my eyes with a look that can only be described as--

I open my mouth to say something super fucking dumb, because this is a stripclub and now isn't the time nor the place. Thankfully she shuts me up by putting a finger against my lips.

"Shhhhhhh!" she shushes me. "You, um... you looked lonely over here so... hi..."

"Hey," I say, trying not to laugh. I think I know what she's doing but let's see how it goes, shall we?

"Do you, um... d-do you come here often...?" she asks.

"Nah, first time," I answer. "How about you?"

She giggles nervously and clings to me with everything she has even if she's trying to do the whole "pretend we don't know each other" thing right now. Which, fuck, I'm kind of into it?

"Um, no," she says, shaking her head. "I... I didn't know how I'd like it at first? I mean, um, b-because you never know what kind of, um... guy? Guys? You... I didn't come here to meet a guy!" she adds, panicked. "B-b-but, um... you look cute and you're really nice and... I like your hair."

"You like my hair?" I ask, trying not to laugh. "Uh, thanks?"

"Shhh, pretend that's a really nice thing to say!" Baby Sis says, giggling nervously. "Please!"

"Dude," I say, failing and laughing this time.

"*Dude!*" she counters, rolling her stupidly fucking sexy eyes at me. Bedroom eyes, for sure. She's got a serious case of bedroom eyes right now.

"Do you want--" I start to say, but I never get to finish that sentence.

"Um, so, I... I was in amateur night earlier, and, um... I can use the private rooms? S-s-sooo... do you want to use one with me?" she asks.

I stare at her because I've been waiting for this moment to come for the past two hours and I'm stuck between immediately saying yes or pretending like I haven't actually been waiting for this moment for two hours so I don't seem too desperate, you know?

Life is fucking hard, man.

"Okay you can say yes now," Baby Sis says, coaching me.

"Wait, what if I say no?" I counter, smirking at her.

"Don't do that!" she says, eyes wide, alarmed. "Umm... wait, I mean, you can say no if you want, but... if you say yes it'll be nice?"

"It'll be nice, will it?" I ask, teasing her.

"If you're going to tease me I'll just go in a private room by myself!" she says, huffing and puffing up her chest and holy fuck her eyes are up here but I can't stop staring down there.

It takes her a second to realize it, but then--

"Are you staring at my boobs?" she asks, head tilted cutely to the side.

"...Yup..." I reluctantly admit.

"You, um... you can stare at them more in a private room, you know?"

"Yeah?"

"Uh huh..."

"Well, fuck," I say, as if that's the thing that convinces me. "By all means..."

"Yay!" she says, excited. "I did it."

"I don't want to ruin this for you but I don't think a stripper would say yay after convincing a guy to go to a private room with her."

"...Shhhhhh..." she mumbles, shoving a finger against my lips again.

She takes my hand in hers and lifts me up from the booth. Everyone else is busy doing their own thing now, Olly's playing some nerdy fantasy card game with Hannah, Chloe's forcing Sam and Amelia to dance, Jenny and Clarissa are doing who the fuck knows what but they look like they're having fun? Lance is surrounded by strippers who may or may not be helping him study. The romance book club girls are excitedly talking about the stripper romance novella again.

And... Teddy and Angela are missing but no one else seems to have noticed yet...

Don't worry, bro. I'll keep your secret. I'm busy anyways.

Baby Sis tries to pretend she's not eager as hell by walking slowly but she keeps giving herself away, squeezing my hand tight, picking up the pace and then slowing down when she realizes it as we walk down the hall to the back rooms and--

Time to find out what all the fuss is about, I guess?

Hell yeah.

HER FIRST LAP DANCE...

Episode 177

CHARLOTTE

I t takes me a second but I belatedly realize Hunter's never been in the back room of a stripclub before.

I have, though? I mean, I went with Hannah and that was different, but still!

I don't know why this makes me feel better because it's kind of a weird thing to feel good about but as we walk up to the counter where the man who keeps guard of the private rooms and collects money is sitting, well... I think this is my time to shine?

I just feel a little more confident and excited knowing that I kind of know what to do and Hunter doesn't and I can tease him a little this time instead of him teasing me?

"You're back," the man says, recognizing me. "Gonna guess this isn't a girl talk moment this time?"

"Um, no," I say, anxious, shaking my head. "I, um... this is..."

Hunter blinks and I blink and the man blinks because I don't know what to say anymore, because--

"Um, this is my boyfriend but I'm pretending he's *not* my boyfriend and... I w-want to give him a lap dance if that's okay?"

"You definitely came to the right place," the man says, laughing. "Look, you don't have to explain anything to me. It takes all sorts, yeah?"

"Oh, okay," I say, nodding. "Um, so... this cute nice boy who is definitely not my boyfriend, um... wait what do we do now?"

I felt confident before but my confidence is taking a turn for the worse with every passing second.

"Bella's got you covered for the usual," the man says, smirking at me and then to Hunter. "Look, I'm not gonna get bent out of shape if you don't tip, but it's a nice thing to do for the friends that take care of you, yeah?"

"Oh, right!" I say, nodding. "Umm..."

I think I left my money in my bag back in the showroom and I know that's kind of dumb and I shouldn't just leave my stuff laying around like that but I forgot and--

"Usually the guy offers to pay," the man says. "That's you, pal. The *not* boyfriend."

"Yeah, okay," Hunter says, and turning to me, he adds. "Dude, I know I wrote about stripclubs but I've literally never been to one. Is this good research or what?"

"Um, if you want it to be good research I think you need to get a lap dance from an actual stripper, though?" I point out. "Also please don't do that."

"Some couples like to do it together?" the man offers, winking at us.

"...I don't want to be that guy but I'd totally be down to watch you get a lap dance from a stripper," Hunter says, sounding both reluctant and somehow not reluctant at the same time.

"Noooo, you're getting a lap dance from *me* and that's it!" I say, giggling. "No other lap dances are happening tonight."

"Sure," he says, kissing my cheek.

Hunter tips the nice man and he says we can have three songs in the room at the end of the hall on the right. Someone'll knock when our time's almost up. Need more time? Come back and see what he can do for us, but, um... I think three songs is enough? How long is that?

I didn't bring my notebook and I don't have my phone either and I don't even know what I'm about to do, but, um...

"I know you two are dating. Or not," the man adds, snickering. "But keep it professional, alright? Save the full experience for back home, pal. Don't get your girl in trouble."

Hunter nods. He looks very disappointed to have to agree to this, but he nods. It's okay, Hunter. I have plans. I think I have plans. I'm going to try something, at least!

I'm g-going to, um...

We head to the room at the end of the hall on the right. The door's already open. I step in and pull Hunter in behind me and we close and lock the door and then--

Before he can do or say anything else or look at me or, you know... just anything. He doesn't have time for a single thing because I push him into the comfy leather bench seat at one end of the room, sort of hard and hopefully assertive. He bounces a couple times, caught off guard, staring up at me, mouth open, looking at me as if he can't believe I, Baby Sis, just did that.

I did, though. I did it, Hunter! *Oh ho ho...*

Just wait until you see what I do next, Hunter.

HUNTER

Holy fucking shit, my stepsister's on fire tonight. Damn, Baby Sis. I love it...

As soon as we step into the private booth, one song ends and another starts, meaning we have three songs, right?

I have no idea what that means exactly, because who

knows what songs are going to play and how long they'll be, but by my super rough calculations we have, like, what, six to nine minutes?

Just kind of guessing here, but seeing as stripclubs apparently do things by the dance, I'd be willing to bet they aim for the low end of that number, also. It makes good business sense, you know?

Why the fuck am I thinking about this shit when I'm hard as hell and finally alone with the girl of all my dreams? No fucking idea.

Anyways, while I'm wasting time thinking about a bunch of stupid bullshit regarding song length, Baby Sis takes control, shoves me into the leather-cushioned bench at one end of our private room, and--

That first part is sexy as fuck which is one of the reasons she's on fire at the moment. Hot as hell, for real.

The second thing she does, though? Uh, not so much but it's amusing so it's cool.

The girls put their regular clothes on after their amateur night dances so she's just wearing jeans and a plain tee. What's underneath is anyone's guess, but I feel like I have a real good idea judging by what I saw on stage. Except, you know, she's currently struggling to remove her clothes as quickly as possible so...

My stepsister flails around in the room, arms stuck in her shirt, most of it above her head while it refuses to actually come off. On the plus side, fuck yeah, she's wearing that pink and black lace bra she wore on stage so I'm distracted by that instead of the fact that she's trapped inside her shirt.

She changes things up to move things along and kind of half bends over, partially crouches, stretching her shirt with her arms to unbutton and unzip her jeans and--

"...Do you need help?" I ask, choking on a laugh.

"N-nooo!" she pants, kicking off her shoes. She got those off easily enough, at least. "Um, wait, maybe?"

I swoop into action like a goddamn stripclub superhero or something and my special ability is, uh... I mean, it's just taking off her shirt. There's no actual superpowers involved, but I wanted to do this as cool and dramatically as possible. I grab one side of her shirt and then the other and tug it up, helping her remove another article of clothing if you count her shoes.

"...Thanks!" she says, standing tall, pretending none of that happened.

I'm pretty willing to believe it because, like I said, her bra is fucking sexy as hell and I get to stare at her breasts nearly spilling out of the thing as she quickly bends over and works at taking her pants off.

Once she's done with that, well...

It's just me, fully clothed, and her in some stupidly attractive lingerie ensemble she somehow managed to sneak past me for who knows how long. It's here now, though. She's here and she's wearing it. And I plan on taking full advantage of both those facts.

After she kicks her feet up to take off her socks, I reach out to grab her and pull her into my lap. Fuck the lap dance, yo. I don't even care. All I want to do right now is--

"W-wait!" Charlotte squeaks, snatching my hands away from her hips. "Um, excuse me, there's *rules*, Hunter!"

Look, I was about to sit her on my lap, shove my hand in the front of her panties, and see how fast I could get her off with my fingers, but now I'm waiting, I guess?

"Why?" I ask, my brain stuck in a temporary feedback loop at the moment. Wait, but, I want to, but, wait, but...

"Um, because?" she answers.

"Is that an actual reason, though?" I ask, hoping I can persuade her otherwise.

"...Yes," she says, so I guess that's that. Fuck. "Um, the rule is... you... you can *touch*, alright?"

"Definitely planning on it," I tell her, fully onboard with

this rule. I start to, you know, do the touching thing, ready to push past the waistband of her lacy lingerie panties again, when--

"W-wait *again!*" she says, giggling. "You, um... you *can* touch, b-but... only from the waist up. Oh, and no grabbing or pulling or... um, yes. Don't do that, alright? I want to make you feel good..."

"Look, I'm not saying I'm not onboard with your rules," I say, attempting to compromise because my dick is hard and I want to shove it inside her so fucking bad right now. I wasn't planning on it yet, but come on, I'm doing my best over here. "But what if we, you know... *don't* do that and instead I do this..."

Which, again, is my third and apparently final attempt at teasing her clit with my fingertip until she cums hard in my lap.

She smacks my forearm before I even get an inch under her panties and artfully pulls my hand away, holds it up, and shakes her head at it.

"No, be good," she says, speaking to my hand instead of me.

To be fair, she's sitting in my lap facing away from me so I kind of get it. Also somehow this is still insanely hot and my erection isn't letting up anytime soon.

"Fine," I grunt. "Have it your way. But--"

"Shhh," she mumbles, leaning back against me, pushing her shoulders against my chest. "No buts. Just, um... you can do *this*, alright?"

She takes my hands and holds them in hers as the first song plays through a speaker somewhere up above. Teasing me, showing me what I can do, she slides my hands up her sides, then along the front of her stomach, and finally to the bottom of her breasts. She leaves me like that, letting me cup her smooth curves and her soft lacy bra in my hands.

Alright, so, yes, if I can't do what I initially wanted to do, this is a pretty great second option.

I start to squeeze because I'm dumb and already forgot half of her lap dance rule. Look, I'm seriously fucking struggling here and there's a serious lack of blood flowing to my brain if you know what I mean? It's taking a hard-earned detour to somewhere halfway up my body that's desperately throbbing and ready to explode at any second.

Baby Sis grinds in my lap, pressing against my cock, sliding up and down, my heart racing, my erection pounding.

"Nuh uh," she says, just that, not making me stop but reminding me of the rules.

I ease up, no longer squeezing, simply holding, touching, feeling.

And then she gets to work...

CHARLOTTE

"Private rooms are where the magic happens," Bella told me earlier after her dance. "Which is why you need to set the scene, take control, and make sure you get what you want out of it. Rule number one is the most important. No touching below the waist. It sends a clear message and sets a boundary. Not only that, but everyone always wants what they can't have. If you tell your boy he isn't allowed to do something, he's going to want it even more. Once you get him home, the only thing he's going to want to do is touch you down there. Trust me on this. You'll thank me later."

And--

"While rule number one is absolute. You can give rule number two more wiggle room if you want. No squeezing, groping, grabbing, whatever. Remember, *you're* in control, honey. If you let him think you aren't, he'll get cocky. Now, you're allowed to let this one slide if you think he's doing it on accident. No full on groping allowed, but if you're riding his lap and his eyes are clenched shut in ecstasy or if they're wide open and glued to yours because he can't look away, well... things happen and he might use more force than he means to. It's basic male instinct to want to thrust when the situation calls for it, and you're going to be doing your damnedest to make him think what you're doing calls for it, understand? If that happens and you want to keep control, what you do is take his hands in yours and first pull back, make him realize what he's doing, and *then* you repeat exactly what he was doing already while letting him know that you're in control of the situation instead of him. He'll get the picture. Trust me. They always do."

I asked her what happens then and what do I do after that? Bella just said, um...

"You'll know what to do. It's not hard. Everyone knows, honey. Just do what feels right and go with it."

Right, okay, so, um...

The first song plays in the private room and at first I don't know what I'm doing but I know the rules and I told Hunter and he's doing really good at following them so far. I still don't fully know what a lap dance involves exactly or how I'm supposed to do one, but I'm in his lap already, so... yes.

I grind back and forth, because I really like feeling him under me, his, um... hard, throbbing, gently thrusting... *you know...*

It's at this moment I realize I *do* know what to do because I kind of maybe accidentally did it already once before?

Not recently. But in the hot tub the first time Hunter and I were, um... ever in a hot tub. And I ended up in his lap on accident and I was excited and everything felt so good and I thought the, um... the prominent hardness pressing into me was Hunter's knee, and I was *so so so so so close* that I just wanted to...

Exactly!

Which, um, the way I'm feeling, I really want to do that

right now, too. What Bella said earlier makes a whole lot of sense all of a sudden.

I also want more, but I don't want to break the rules because I'm the one who made them in the first place, you know? I shift my butt so I'm pressing against the best spot for maximum grindability, Hunter's hardness straining at the front of his pants. I fit my body perfectly against him, my thighs with his, my, um... the bottom front of my panties pressing directly against his bulging erection. Every time I slide back and forth, even though we're separated by layers of clothes, I feel him throbbing and pounding against my pussy.

It... it feels really really nice? I think that's the point Bella was trying to make, too.

Somehow I really do know what to do even if I didn't know it at first.

While I tease and torment Hunter, the first song coming to an end, I lean forward slightly and arch my back. He squeezes a little too hard, either from not wanting me to go or to keep his hands in place while I push away slightly. I let him hold me for a second because I have something else to do, which, um... you know, I reach back, unclasp my lacy bra, and slide the straps off my shoulders.

Once I'm done, I lean back against him again, a little harder than before. Hunter groans as I grind my body against his pulsing hardness. I reach up and take his hands in mine and use them to... to help me take my bra off. When it's most of the way off, I let it go, watching it slip to the floor, and then I softly slide his hands back to where they just were.

I move him up, pressing his palms against my bare breasts. Gasping and moaning when my nipples firm up, pressing between his fingers, I slide and grind and oh gosh this feels incredible...

Hunter keeps holding my breasts for a few seconds longer as the second song begins to play. It's a faster song this time, a little more going on, and I match my "dance" in his lap with the tempo of the music. Quicker, quicker, sliding and rocking and grinding against him, I can feel his erection desperately tenting the front of his pants. It's so hard and hot and I kind of really want to feel him inside me right now but I don't know if we're even allowed to do that here and, um... Bella's rules, right?

This is it. If I can do this, I can do, um... maybe anything but I don't know if I could *actually* do anything, but, um...

Hunter's going to be mine forever after this? Oh, and when we make love later it's going to be amazing.

Wait, um, m-make love? Oh gosh. I really just thought that and I don't know if I should've but... yes please?

Hunter wraps one arm around me, trying to stick to the rules, not quite holding me but, um... pretty close? His left hand presses lightly against my right breast as his fingers wrap around my curves. His right hand slips low, like he's knowingly going to break the rules now, but he stops right at the top of my panties. He spreads his fingers, touching every inch of my lower stomach he possibly can.

...If he were inside me right now and holding me like this it'd feel amazing...

Just to, um... to tease him a little bit more...

"You... you can't touch below my waist, remember?" I say, whispering a reminder to him as I lean back, turning my head so our cheeks touch.

"I remember," he groans, letting out a strangled grunt as I grind against him harder. "Fuck!" he gasps. "Are you..." he moans, losing track of that thought for a second as I ride in his lap. "Are you *trying* to make me cum in my pants?"

"...Maybe?" I offer, a silly purr of a giggle. "If you do, um... it's okay, okay? I... I'd like it a lot..."

"Not sure I have much of a choice in the matter at the moment," Hunter says, trying to make light of a sexy situation.

Oh gosh yes please I want you to cum for me...

I don't say that out loud because I'm trying to be sexy and confident right now but, um... still, oh gosh yes please I want you to cum for me, Hunter!

"I'm going to hold your hand," I tell him, pressing one hand over his as he does his best to stay out of my panties. "No moving it, alright? Promise me, please."

"Yes," he grunts, ragged and rough. "I promise."

"Good," I purr. "Now, um... *I'm* going to move it a little, but that's *me*, alright? So, um... you don't move on your own or we have to stop and that would be sad."

"Sure?" Hunter agrees, not knowing what he's getting himself into.

...I'm so ready for this, though...

I hold the back of his hand and gently dip it beneath the front of my panties. I slide his middle finger just above my, um... the hood of my clit? *There.* I think he realizes what I'm doing because his hand tenses up and I think maybe he regrets agreeing to this so easily but he already did so, you know... it's too late to take it back, Hunter!

The second song continues, quick and heady, and I don't know exactly how long it is but it's plenty long enough and somehow not nearly long enough. It seems like it goes on forever but when it ends it's like it was only playing for a few seconds. I gently press into Hunter's lap, working him up even more, his left hand cupping one of my breasts while his right hand dips into my panties and I, um...

I use his middle finger for my pleasure, two of my fingers pressed against the bottom of his, pushing his fingertip against the absolute upper limits of the hood of my... sweet juicy pearl? I mean, that's what's going on right now, pretty much. I'm sweet *and* juicy and... *uh huh...*

I grind my body against my stepbrother. I can feel his cock desperately trying to drill through our clothes so he can bury himself inside me. Every so often I feel him forcefully reminding himself not to move his hand so he can keep his fingers just above my clit and--

...I've never felt more alive, sexy, and confident in my entire life and I absolutely love every second of this...

I'm not done yet, though. We have one more song to go.

HOTTER, HARDER, FASTER, MORE

Episode 178

HUNTER

I'm on the brink of death, or pleasure overload, and the third song's only just begun. Fuck me, man. What the hell is going on and how did my stepsister get so goddamn good at giving a lap dance?

To be fair, she's always been pretty great in general, despite what she seems to think of herself. Reactive as fuck, moving her body perfectly to bring us together in combined passion, and... yeah, everything about her hits all my buttons and drives me wild all the time.

This is on a whole new level, though. Holy fucking shit.

While she completely fucking uses and abuses me for her own pleasure, teasing the fuck out of every inch of my body in ways I never realized I wanted before, the third song starts to pick up and she suddenly stops.

She leaps out of my lap like I'm on fire and for a fraction of a second I think I broke one of her rules and this is my punishment? Except immediately after she jumps up, she spins around and hops back in. She's facing me this time and

I don't know if this is better or worse because there's absolutely no way I can touch her the way I was before.

Except *this* way she can grind against me even harder, more in control than ever, and holy fuck she does that and ramps my dick up to eleven. I was a ten before, completely ready to burst, but now I'm surprised I haven't already.

Charlotte takes my hands in hers and brings them to her cheeks, staring me hard in the eyes. Her nose pushes against mine, cute and hot at the same time. She looks into my fucking soul, wide-eyed and excited, as she forcefully grinds back and forth in my lap like she wants me to cum right here and now.

"If, um... if you don't finish soon, I will..." she mumbles, holding my cheeks in her palms, sliding back and forth across my excruciatingly hard erection.

"Is that a threat or a promise?" I ask, trying to tease her back a little.

"Shhh, no talking," she says, pretending to kiss me but pulling her lips away at the last second.

I closed my eyes and everything, got ready for it, and when her lips never touched mine I started to push my way towards her but she just leans back, pulls away, and... fuck me, man...

"No, um... no kissing, either," she says, giggling, torturous.

"Fine," I groan as she expertly works my lap. "But if you finish first, we're leaving. Immediately. And I'm dragging you back to my room and neither of us is sleeping tonight. I don't care if we both have class in the morning. I get to have my way with you all damn night, Baby Sis. Understand?"

"Okay," she says, smiling sweetly. "But I won't."

It's at that moment I realize how much I fucked up...

Harder, faster, she bucks against my lap, grinding her panty-covered pussy against my throbbing hard cock. I can practically fucking feel her wetness soaking through my pants and I'm pretty sure there's going to be a wet spot when

I get up but I don't even fucking care. I don't have time to think about it, don't have time to even consider what's going to happen when we get out of this room, because she knows full well what she's doing, how to do it, and--

It's like a two-pronged force of attack here. She slides her lace-covered lower lips up and down across my shaft, except as she gets to the edge, near the head of my erection, she nudges herself a little lower, pushing against me as if I'm going to *finally* get my chance to thrust inside her. Obviously I can't. There's clothes in the way. But that's what it *feels* like and my goddamn traitorous hard-on is having a fucking field day with that one.

I lose my own bet about five seconds after I make it and it's both the hottest thing that's ever happened to me and I feel slightly disappointed at the same time. Like, come on, bro? Couldn't you have held off for a little bit longer? Not that I'm complaining too much, because holy fucking shit I can't stop now that I've started and, yeah... there's going to be a huge mess to deal with but I'll figure that shit out later.

It's my stepsister's fault and she damn well knows it.

Anyways--

The third song's still playing and Baby Sis wants hers too. I'm pretty sure she can tell what just happened without me saying it. Maybe the fact that my eyes rolled into the back of my head as I let out a loud moan helps. Maybe it's more the fact that she's now intimately aware of what it feels like for my shaft to go over the edge and release everything inside her.

It's probably because I think I accidentally said "Fuck" out loud in the most incriminating way possible, but it could be a combination of all of the above.

When I regain partial control of myself and look her in the eyes again she's staring at me with the most intense and sexy look possible. Her eyes are fucking gleaming, nearly demonic, excited at what she just made me do. Also, you know, a few seconds later her own eyes roll into the back of her head as she slams and grinds against my lap, finding her own finish.

I hold her cheeks and watch her embrace her pleasure, seeing every moment of her ecstasy as it unfurls. It's fucking mesmerizing. I could watch her like this all day long. I really want to one day.

When she comes down from her orgasmic high, we both look at each other, just kind of staring soulfully into each other's eyes. Our mouths open and I think we're both about to say something and the thing I'm about to say is probably not something I should say in a private room in a stripclub while getting a lap dance but whatever, I don't even fucking care anymore.

None of that has a chance to happen because someone knocks at our door before we put thoughts into words.

"Time's almost over," a guy says. "Finish up."

Baby Sis stares at the door, eyes wide. She looks like she only just realized what we just finished doing and where we did it. It's somehow adorable and hot at the same time. I fucking love it.

"Ummm... I need to put my clothes back on?" she mumbles, giggling nervously.

"Probably a good idea," I say with a smirk. "I'll help you take them off again later, don't worry."

"Will you?" she teases back, finally managing to wink at me with one eye instead of her usual two-eyed wink blink.

Shit, she's getting too good at this.

My stepsister pulls on her pants and gets into her shirt a lot easier this time. I help her find her shoes, which somehow ended up under our leather-backed bench. And, you know, we finish in the nick of time.

Right as the third song ends, we unlock and open the door to let an actual working stripper and her man for the next six to nine minutes into the room. I don't recognize the girl, but she winks at Baby Sis who immediately turns bright, beet red.

I take my girlfriend's hand in mine and we head down the hall and out to the showroom to regroup with our friends.

...And, yeah, I need a quick trip to the bathroom to clean up after what happened, but whatever, don't even get me started...

Also halfway down the hall, another door quickly opens and Angela and Teddy step out. Teddy looks... interesting... I don't actually know what that look on his face is about yet. Angela is... way more cheerful and giddy than usual which is saying a lot because she's always fucking cheerful and giddy.

Holy fuck, Teddy. What'd you do? Your girl is getting even worse. You're literally creating a monster here, bro. Fuck.

"Ummmm..." Baby Sis mumbles upon seeing the two of them together.

"...Yeah," I agree, sighing and shaking my head.

Angela stops, freezes, stares at us. Teddy looks guilty as hell for whatever he's done. I can't save you now, bro. Your secret's out.

"I... I d-didn't tell him!" Baby Sis quickly says to Angela.

"Wait, what?" I counter, glaring at her. "You didn't tell me what?"

"Um, nothing?" she says, lying her sexy fucking black and pink lace panty-wearing ass off.

"I accidentally told Hunter!" Teddy says, giving himself in. Dude, come on...

"Wait, you did?!" Angela gasps, staring at him, somehow looking cheerfully betrayed. I don't even know how that's a thing but she makes it work.

"Angela told me too, Teddy," Baby Sis informs him. "It's okay."

"Babe, it's not, like, *okay*..." Angela huffs. "I mean, it was totally supposed to be a secret, you know?"

"Look, about that," I snap back. "What are you doing to Teddy and why are you trying to ruin his life?"

Easy question. Let's hear the answer, you succubus.

"I'm not *trying* to ruin his life!" Angela counters, aghast. "Um, Teddy, am I ruining your life? I'm sorry."

"No, not really?" Teddy says with a shrug. "I just feel bad sneaking around, you know?"

"Do you, like... *not* want to sneak around then?" Angela asks, subtle as a fucking brick that just smashed through a convenience store window.

Don't do it, Teddy. Don't give in. You deserve better. Also Jenny will kill her.

"It's not that I want to stop," Teddy says, conflicted. "I really enjoy sleeping with you. Like, seriously, it's the best sleep I've ever had in my entire life."

"What about the shower, though?" Baby Sis asks, letting that piece of information into the wild. "That, um... that was..."

"Nothing happened!" Angela squeals. "We, um... Teddy just washed my back and I totally washed his and now we're both squeaky clean and that's what's important, don't you think?"

"Is it, though?" I ask, totally not buying it.

"I have felt pretty clean since then?" Teddy offers, oblivious. "It's really hard to scrub my back sometimes."

"Look, what if you just, I don't fucking know... stop sneaking around, but *don't* stop doing what you're doing? There's got to be a word for it... what's the word I'm thinking of... Baby Sis, help me out here?"

My stepsister stares at me like I just threw her under a literal bus. I don't even know why. She's the one that knew about Teddy and Angela and never told me. I mean, I knew and never told her either, but that's different. I was sworn to secrecy to save Teddy's life! My stepsister, though? Not so much. I refuse to believe it.

"I think it's okay to be friends," Baby Sis says with a nod of approval. "Maybe it's better if you're more open about that? Like, um... I don't know how, though. Rules? I think rules are good. Rules help a lot with a lot of things so maybe you should have rules and, um... is... is that it?"

She asks this while looking at me for confirmation and I don't know how to let her down gently and tell her that, no, that isn't it. These two should just fuck, finally confirm their friends with benefits, dating, whatever the fuck relationship they want to have, and be done with it.

But yeah, sure, friends. Let's go with that.

"Wait, what kind of rules, babe?" Angela asks.

"Can we talk about this later?" Teddy says. "I think we're in the way."

"You totally are but I'm enjoying this so take your time," Ruby says from behind us.

"I have no idea what's going on," Lance adds, apparently with Ruby.

"I'm saving you, sweetie," Ruby tells him. "Otherwise you'll get taken for everything you're worth."

"Oh, cool, but, uh... I thought these rooms were for lap dances?"

"Do you *want* a lap dance, baby?" Ruby asks, smirking at him. "That can definitely be arranged..."

"Oh oh oh, I want a lap dance!" Angela says, waving her hand in the air. "Me me me! Ruby!"

"You're funny," Ruby says, giggling. "Love it! You and Clarissa need to come visit again. Girl's night?"

"Totally!"

"Um, can I come?" Baby Sis asks.

"Charlie, yes!"

"Dude, why do the girls like the stripclub more than us?" I ask Teddy, because come the fuck on, what's even happening here. This has been going on all night.

"I think it's probably a combination of feeling empowered and also knowing their worth," Teddy says, profound as fuck. "To be honest, I never really thought about it much before, but stripclubs seem to be a good way for women to flaunt their bodies safely, or hopefully as safely as possible, while still maintaining full control of the situation. I can see how that would be fun, you know? We don't have to deal with the same issues, Jacksy. Like, we can walk around shirtless whenever we want and I've never felt unsafe doing it, but I don't think women can usually walk around in almost nothing without feeling anxious."

"It's super true," Angela says, nodding along. "But I'd feel totally safe walking around in almost nothing around you, Teddy. So, like, if you ever want to help me feel empowered and sexy, well..."

Teddy's inner feminist is trying to wrestle its way through that proposition and I think there's steam coming out of his ears. It's cool, bro. I get it. Don't even worry. Just go with it, man.

"Anyways, move your cute little tushies," Ruby says. "Lance! Let's hang out. Then I'll bring you back to study. If you want to sneak out the back when the other girls aren't looking, I've got your back, sweetie. Just say the word."

"Ruby's so nice!" Angela says, shifting to the side to let her ex-cheerleader stripper friend do her thing.

Lance apologizes and sneaks past us and before they even get into a room he's saying, "That'd be great, actually. Maybe after I finish my coffee?"

"Sure, just sit by my stage when my next set is up and stare at my tits a little to make it believable. I'll bring you back for another dance and sneak you out afterwards, okay?"

"Okay, thanks a lot, Ruby."

I literally have no idea what's going on or why it's happening but yeah, apparently this is my life now.

"Can we go, um... sit and finish reading the stripper romance novella with the book club girls now?" Baby Sis asks. "It seemed really good. I like it so far."

"Sure," I say, grinning at her. "Yeah, it's cool, huh? Not that realistic, but I'm into it."

"It's a novella, though," she points out. "Do they get married and have a baby at the end?"

"Uh, probably not..." I admit. "I think sometimes in shorter romance stories they just have that whole happy for now thing, right? Like, it's not a full on happily ever after ending, but they're happy and you know they're going to keep going in the future, so yeah."

"Wait, you're reading a *stripper* romance?!" Angela asks, excited, coming over and stealing my girlfriend away. "Can I read it, babe? If it's short I think I can make it through. It's just that Joanna always picks those really long books, you know? Like, totally way too long. But, like... I could *totally* read a short book about a stripper falling in love. Do strippers fall in love? If I were a stripper, I think I could fall in love, but maybe only with, like, the bad boy but not really that bad, you know? He'd have to actually be a nice guy but he looks like he could totally be a bad boy in the right circumstances, right? Oh and he's a football player and he's hot and respectful and I never knew I was into that, but, Charlie, I'm *totally* into it, you know? Is that a thing?"

"Um, the hero in the novella isn't a football player but he was kind of a bad boy?" Baby Sis offers. "He, um... they knew each other before and he shows up at the club she's working at when his friend is having a bachelor party there and--"

The head cheerleader literally grabs Charlotte's hand and tugs her down the hall without me. What the fuck? Now it's just me and Teddy standing together.

"Look," Teddy says. "Jacksy, I know this looks really bad, but nothing happened, you know?"

"You don't have to explain anything to me, man," I tell him. "I understand."

"Oh, good," he says, relieved. "Wait, you do? Because I don't."

"Sure, it's easy. Just answer this one question: Do you want to rail the shit out of Angela, yes or no?"

"I mean, it's not actually *that* easy, is it?" Teddy counters. "Clearly she's beautiful. The temptation is there, right? I'd be stupid not to recognize how attractive she is. But, uh... *rail?* I don't know if that's the word I'd use. Also we're just friends, and I don't think it'd be appropriate given the circumstances, so..."

"What if you ask her out?"

"We go out already?"

"I meant on a date, dude. Come on."

"That might be awkward, don't you think? I mean, what if it doesn't work out and we aren't friends anymore?"

"Teddy," I say, trying to pinpoint exactly where the issue is. "Do you think Angela wants to be your friend right now?"

"...Yes?" he answers, confused. "Wait, shit, are you saying she doesn't want to be my friend? I don't really get it then. Is she doing all this just to screw with me? Because she seems like she's having fun too, so I don't know, man. I think we're friends already?"

"Nah, nevermind," I say, shaking my head and swaggering down the hall. "Forget about it, bud. I didn't mean anything by it."

"How's your night going, by the way?" Teddy asks, just checking in. What a bro, am I right?

"Really great, man," I say with a grin. "Best night of my life so far."

"Damn, sounds nice!"

"You having fun, too?"

"Yeah, I am."

"Cool, cool."

And... there we have it. The night continues, Baby Sis and I hang out with the book club girls. Olly plays his nerdy card game with the cute nerd girl with the booty of his dreams or whatever. Sam teases the fuck out of Amelia with Chloe's help. Lance sneaks out of the club with Ruby's help, much to the disappointment of Gia. And Jenny and Clarissa keep buying each other mocktails and telling each other how pretty they are.

It's a pretty great night. I have a nice time.

Unfortunately my stepsister passes out on the ride home, just completely fucking exhausted and spent, but it's cool.

I carry her to my room and Teddy helps me open the door and then totally fucking caves and takes Angela back to his room to sleep which is the weirdest shit ever but who even cares anymore.

And...

I gently strip off Charlotte's clothes, stuff her in some pajamas, tuck her into bed, and watch her sleep for a minute before starting to do the same.

As soon as I try to get into bed next to her, she starts wriggling around. At first I think she's having a bad dream or something, but, nah, not even close?

At around the same time as I pull the covers back to hop in bed next to her, she finishes her squirming and neatly pushes her pajama shorts onto the floor. Dude, I literally just put those on you!

And... fuck me...

"*Noooooo,*" she mumbles, slowly blinking her eyes open, staring up at me as I stand at the edge of my bed. "You *promised,* Hunter..." she murmurs, sleepy and cute. And then she says the words to end all words. "...I want you to make love to me..."

I'm pretty sure she's like half asleep and barely realizes what she's saying but she's so fucking beautiful right now. She lazily reaches for my hand, holds it lightly in hers, and tugs me into the bed with her.

Without missing a beat, pulling me on top of her, shifting me between her legs, she fumbles with the waistband of my pajama pants until she has them low enough that she can reach for my aching cock, and--

CHARLOTTE

It's, um... it's late and I'm half asleep and I know we're in the dorms again, back in Hunter's room, in his bed, but I had this sudden, nagging feeling that... I don't know *what* yet, but... I'm forgetting something?

I lay there, in between falling back to sleep or waking up, at least for a little bit. It could go either way and I don't know which is which yet, but then I feel Hunter, the weight of him ready to settle into bed next to me, and it all comes back to me.

Kind of. Um, I'm still barely awake and I don't know what I'm saying but--

"...I want you to make love to me..."

I don't think I could've said those words like that if I were fully awake and aware of what I'm doing, but right now, right here, after what we did tonight, they're the easiest words in the world to say.

I blindly reach for his hand and pull him into bed. I had shorts on but I don't anymore. Hunter has pants on. Why? We need to get rid of those, please. Okay, um, there, good, thank you.

I weakly stuff my fingers into the waistband of his pants, my hands forgetting how to work for a second because I'm barely awake. I wrestle with his pajamas, tugging them low enough that I feel a sudden *pop* when his apparently already ready erection bounces free.

Yay... that's for me...

I reach for him without thinking and wrap my fingers around it, lazily stroking him even though he really doesn't need much help getting hard right now. It's just nice. I'm sleepy and this is nice and I like it and--

Hunter settles between my thighs and leans in close, kissing me softly on the forehead. I let out a little mewl, happy and content. He's so close and I'm still holding him so I guide him towards me without thinking about it. Slow, easy, the head of Hunter's cock dips between my lower lips, fitting in perfectly.

I tell him as much as he kisses my forehead, then lower, lips against my closed eyelids, my nose, a gentle peck on my lips

"There," I say, eyes shut, smiling softly. "Perfect."

Hunter pushes in further while I hold him tight, hugging him, not wanting to open my eyes again just yet.

It's hard to explain but I feel like I'm halfway between sleeping and waking up and everything feels so soft and fuzzy and warm and nice?

That's what it feels like when he sinks all the way inside me, too. It's slow and smooth, a deliberate, inch by inch sensation as he fills me, satisfying my sleepy needs.

Hunter stays like that as soon as he's all the way inside. I don't really know what I'm doing right now but I think my body does? I whimper, excited, and kiss him, and he kisses me back. I don't do it on purpose, don't mean to, but it feels so good, feels really really nice, and I start to clench and squeeze against him as he stays in me, deep and full.

After a few moments like that, Hunter slides out. Not all the way, but maybe, um... halfway? My eyes have been closed this entire time, like maybe I'm dreaming all this but I know I'm not. He pushes back in, taking his time, slow and steady. I squeeze against him again as soon as he starts to fill me, to make love to me.

It's the easiest thing I've ever done and it feels incredible.

We come together like that, in, out, slow, taking our time, like we have it all, all the time in the world that we could ever want; seconds, minutes, hours, days. Hunter slips into a perfect rhythm, in for a few seconds, and then out. I whimper and squeeze against him, clutching his shaft, holding him tight inside me for as long as I can. He kisses me and I try to kiss him back but it's a little hard and I'm distracted by how good this feels right now.

I don't know when exactly it starts, but suddenly it doesn't just feel good, it feels amazing. I open my mouth wider, gasping and moaning. Hunter moves faster, just a little bit, not too much but enough to make it feel that much different, that much more passionate and intense.

I cum before I know it, without even realizing it's starting or happening at first, and I feel my reinvigorated wetness making it even easier for him to slide inside me. Smooth and slippery and perfect, Hunter makes love to me, on and on, keeping my orgasm going, keeping the height of my passion at its peak for as long as possible.

It's like one long, continuous moment of ecstasy. I don't know if this is just one *O* or a few back to back. It feels like it could be either or maybe both somehow. After a long long time like that, or maybe just a minute, I feel him ready to finish, to fill me, to make love to me and seal our fate.

Bella said he would be mine forever if I followed her rules and I really really want that to be true.

Please, Hunter...

He grunts as he thrusts all the way inside me, wanting to fill me as deeply as possible. I hold him, hugging him gently. I open my eyes and kiss his face, his lips, his cheeks, his everything, as he spills jet after jet of his cum deep inside me.

I can't even think right now. I just want to feel it. I want to love him, to make love to him, to be in love with him. I want to--

Hunter finishes and I can't stop kissing him now. He laughs and I giggle and we cuddle while he's still inside me and I can feel him, fully and completely. I squeeze gently around his softening shaft and he makes it throb and pulse for me. It's fun and sexy and I like it a lot.

I like him a lot.

I...

Hunter helps clean me up after as best he can but I'm already on my way to falling back to sleep after that sexy little detour. I close my eyes and breathe softly and just as I think I'm asleep I feel him cuddle close to me, both of us still pantsless, naked and close.

I like that a lot. I want to be close to him like this, always.

I don't know if it's him, if he actually says it, or if I'm dreaming, but I hear the words perfectly and I hope they're real.

"I love you."

I mumble it back, trying to say it too, but I'm suddenly exhausted, so tired, and I think I fall asleep before I realize it.

I love you, Hunter. I love you so much. I want you to know that.

HUNTER

That was perfect. It was so fucking amazing. It was raw and beautiful and I've never done anything like that before in my entire life.

We just made love. Fully and completely. It felt like everything. It felt perfect.

I curl up next to her, my girlfriend, my stepsister, Baby Sis, Charlotte, the girl I love more than anything.

I don't know why I do what I do next but I just kind of do it and I can't take it back after, so...

"I love you," I say.

She mumbles something in her sleep but who even knows what.

Next time I say it I promise she'll be awake to hear it properly. I want her to know how I feel so fucking bad. I want to say it out loud, so fucking loud, and tell her all the time, and--

I fall asleep with my arms wrapped around her, holding her tight.

I KNEW YOU WERE TROUBLE

Episode 179

CHARLOTTE

"**A**s your legal advisor, I must inform you this is ill-advised," Natalie says, pushing her glasses up her nose and staring at Angela. "The prudent course of action is immediate destruction."

"Noooooooooo," Clarissa croons. "Do we *have* to? It's, like... you know... totally?"

"For sure, babe," Angela agrees, standing tall. "I, for one, want to watch it again. For, you know, strictly professional reasons?"

"Yes! Totally professional!"

"None of what's on this is professional," Natalie informs them, scrunching up her nose. "In fact, it's the opposite. Which is why I still recommend--"

"It doesn't hurt to watch it once, right?" Jenny says with a shrug. "I don't know. I think it's fine, myself."

"Yay! Jenny agrees!" Clarissa says, excitedly hopping up and down.

"Oh oh oh," Angela adds, joining in. "What if we put it in the Vault?"

"Um, what's the vault?" I ask, sitting quietly and trying not to make too much of a fuss.

It's the day after we entered amateur night at the stripclub and, um... basically Natalie confiscated the hidden recording Erica made of us pole dancing. Erica snuck it into Lance's textbook? It was technically her textbook, but she asked Lance to bring it, and...

Basically I think she wanted to blackmail us again? I know she tried it in the past with Angela and Clarissa, and then she tried doing it to me a few weeks ago with the posters and the risque photos she stole off Hunter's phone, and, um... now she did it again at the stripclub?

I kind of agree with Natalie. We should probably destroy this, but also--

"It's *the* Vault, babe," Angela informs me. "It's not just any old vault. It's where we keep all our highly classified and sensitive information related to, you know, cheerleading. If anyone ever gained access to it, like... they could ruin our lives forever. That's how sensitive it is. It's a lot. That's why we put Natalie in charge of it."

"It's a private lockbox at a bank," Natalie says. "While it contains sensitive information, I doubt it would result in anyone's lives being ruined forever. Unless we put this recording there, in which case, yes, you could all find your lives ruined forever in the future. Which is why I *still* insist we--"

"Um, I... I don't want to, um..." I start to say, because I don't want to intrude on highly classified or sensitive cheerleader information, but... "Maybe we can watch it once and decide after?"

"Yes!" Clarissa says, excited. "See? If Charlie thinks it's fine I'm sure it's fine. Right?"

"For sure," Angela agrees. "Totally. Right, Natalie?"

"No, not particularly," Natalie says, sighing. "But we *are* alone and I can't see the harm if the door's locked."

"Heck yeah!" Jenny cries out. "I didn't want to sound too excited earlier because I don't know if my dance was as good as everyone else, but I really want to see it, you know?"

"Same, babe," Angela agrees. "Same."

"Me too!" Clarissa squeals, beyond hyped.

Everyone looks at me and I think I'm supposed to say something, so...

"...I want to see my dance, too?" I offer.

"Let's do it!" Angela says, running off to find whatever needs finding.

Natalie stands there, resolute, fiercely guarding the recording. She's just holding a USB drive with the video on it and not much else, but she looks very stern and authoritative as she does it. I wouldn't want to mess with her right now. I don't think anyone would. Not even Hunter. No teasing allowed here. Nope.

Oh, and... we're in the cheerleader locker room, everything as pink as possible, as usual. The bench I'm sitting on is pink, the concrete floor is pink, the lockers are pink, and--

Angela wheels a TV on a stand into the locker room. The TV *and* the stand are pink. I've never seen a pink TV before and it takes me a second to figure out what it is because of that. But, nope, it's a TV.

"Alright," Angela says, pushing it into place and sitting down quick on a bench so she can watch. "Hit it, Natalie!"

Natalie sighs, clicks her way to the TV stand in her heels, and plugs the USB stick into the TV. A second later she takes the remote from the stand, heads back to where we're eagerly sitting, and, um...

I'm really really excited. I know everyone liked my dance but I want to see it for myself. I wonder what it looked like when my clothes started to rip away?

...Or that'll be super embarrassing to watch but everyone was very nice about it when it happened so I'm sure it's fine...

Anyways, right--

Natalie flicks through the menu and pushes play.

"Whoa," Angela says after we've watched all our dances.

"It was like, good, but... was it sideways for everyone else, too?" Clarissa asks, her head still tilted at an angle.

"I think it's because the camera was in a book?" Jenny offers. "The book was sideways, so... right?"

"I think that's why too," I agree.

"Oh, good," Clarissa says. "I thought maybe I was seeing things. Or maybe, like, the world's *always* sideways for *everyone* but we don't realize it because we see it straight up since *we're* sideways, too?"

"Babe..." Angela says, staring wide-eyed at her friend. "Like, *whoa*. I've never thought about it like that before. It makes sense, though. If the Earth is round and we're on the Earth then, like... sometimes we're sideways..."

"Sometimes we're upside down, too," Clarissa adds, nodding.

"...I d-don't think that's how that works?" I point out. "There's gravity and..."

"It's fine, Charlotte," Jenny says. "They'll be fine in a second. Just let them be."

"That's usually for the best," Natalie agrees. "If I had to guess, they'll be done in--"

She looks at her watch and silently counts down from five. It's at that exact moment the cheerleaders stop worrying about being sideways, upside-down, or at a forty-five degree angle, which apparently makes sense somehow because didn't we learn about right triangles in math class one time?

"So *that's* what those were about!" Clarissa says.

"Totally, babe. For sure," Angela agrees. "But look, like, as fun as it is thinking that maybe instead of being on the bottom during hardcore missionary sex we're *actually* on top because the Earth is, like, upside-down? Let's focus on what's more important right now. Which is how freaking *badass* we were at the stripclub!"

"I know, right!" Clarissa squeals, clapping at least ten times. "It was so fun, too! Oh my gosh, I loved your dance, Charlie! I'm sorry your clothes fell off but it looked totally hot."

"They, um... they were supposed to fall off?" I say. "It was a secret! I planned it. Bella and Saskia helped. I just had to tear them in this one spot and the friction with the pole made them slowly rip away and... yes."

Clarissa nods along, a suspiciously raised eyebrow, like I'm either a sexy mad genius or she's not sure I'm telling the truth. Either way, she gives me a quick thumbs up at the end; full approval.

"Okay, look," Angela says, taking a deep breath. "We should put this to a vote. All in favor of keeping the recording of our total boss bitch badass sexy night at the stripclub in the Vault, say aye!"

"Aye!" Clarissa immediately says.

"Aye, totally," Angela agrees.

...I don't know what to vote for and I don't want to ruin this for anyone because I *do* kind of want a copy to, um... maybe show Hunter later? Except I don't want this to ruin anyone's life, either. That sounds bad. I'm really struggling right now.

Angela and Clarissa look to me and Jenny for hopeful confirmation.

"Okay, what about this?" Jenny says to Natalie. "What if we blur our faces? Someone could edit the recording, right? Oh, while we're at it, maybe they can make it right-side up instead of sideways? That'd be cool."

"...Wait can someone do that?!" Angela asks, super excited. "Yes! Jenny! Babe! You're amazing!"

"Aww, thanks!" Jenny says, giggling. "I try."

Natalie considers it, lips pursed in thought. "It's possible," she reluctantly admits. "The issue is that in order to do it, we'd need to give an outside third-party access to the unedited version, which introduces a liability risk. I'm not sure it's worth it."

"...What if we know someone we trust who can edit it?" I ask.

"*Do* you know someone?"

"Um, no, not really.

"It's a good idea, Charlotte," Jenny says, smiling. "Don't worry about it."

"Um, can I ask a question, though?" Clarissa says, raising her hand high.

"Clarissa," Natalie says with a sigh. "I've told you this before. You don't have to raise your hand to ask me a question. I'm your legal advisor and friend, not a professor."

"Oh, right!" Clarissa says, lowering her hand, happy as ever. "Why do we want to blur our faces? I like my face."

"Such a good point," Angela agrees. "I also like my face. I like Clarissa's face, too. Actually, you know what? Babes, I like *all* our faces. I don't think I can vote in favor of blurring our faces because of that. It seems wrong, am I right?"

Jenny stares at them with something akin to abject exasperation about where to even begin explaining any of this.

I don't know either. Sorry, Jenny.

"I believe the intention behind blurring your faces is to maintain your anonymity and privacy so that if you keep a copy of said video, and it were inadvertently leaked to the public, it would be difficult if not impossible to identify you. This limits the potential for future catastrophe."

Natalie says this with a straight face while Clarissa and Angela nod along, trying to wrap their heads around it.

"Alright, but, like, what about our *voices*?" Angela asks. "Do we have to blur those, too?"

"I also like my voice," Clarissa adds. "I know not everyone agrees, and that's, like, totally fine even if they're wrong, but I think I have a light and endearingly sweet and charming cadence."

"Like, totally, babe," Angela agrees. "For sure. You sound like a beautiful and super hot angel sent straight from heaven."

"Awwwww, babe!"

"...How do you blur a voice?" I ask, hoping someone can help me out here.

"Maybe it's like in those news interviews where they expose the truth behind some secret?" Jenny offers. "They blur their face *and* they use a voice changer to make them sound deep and husky so you can't recognize their voice, either."

"Can we do that but make it sultry and husky?" Angela asks, looking to Natalie for confirmation. "I know what Jenny's talking about but I don't want to sound like a man. Do we get to pick what voice we get?"

"If we do, I want to sound like Taylor Swift," Clarissa says with a nod.

"I'm unsure if that's even remotely possible," Natalie tells them. "If it *is*, I'm positive that modulating your voice to sound like Taylor Swift's introduces even more potential future issues. So, no. I'm sorry, Clarissa. You can't sound like Taylor Swift."

"Darn."

"When do we need to finish voting?" I ask. "I, um... this is too hard. I don't want anyone to have their lives ruined b-but, um... I *do* like my dance..."

"Like, we get it, Charlie," Angela says, reassuringly. "You totally want to show it to Hunter, because, like, who wouldn't? It's basically the easiest way to make him insta-hard, and, like, sometimes that's exactly what you want, right?"

"I usually just flash my boobs or say something about

wanting something in my mouth and that works, but I agree with Angela," Clarissa says.

"I never knew this was a thing I wanted in my life, but now that I do I feel like I've been missing out," Jenny says, brow scrunched up. "What the heck, babes."

"I'll make this easy," Natalie says. "If you can't reach a unanimous decision by the end of today's last class, I'm destroying the recording. This is in the best interests of everyone involved."

"What if it's in my best interest to have a really hot recording of me and Angela dancing at a stripclub so I can instantly make whatever boy I want hard, though?" Clarissa asks. "What then, Natalie?!"

"No," she says, having dealt with the cheerleaders plenty of times before. "You clearly have alternative methods available. You don't need this one."

"Ugh. I hate it when she's right."

"Same, babe," Angela agrees. "Same."

They look to me and Jenny, hopeful, and yet--

As much as I like the idea of having a copy, maybe Natalie's right? We don't even know anyone we can trust who can edit it, so...

I feel bad, but it is what it is.

And so--

HUNTER

"Alright, boys, listen up," Olly says to us during a covert sneaky lunch outside on the front lawn. "Rumor has it the exploitative blackmail video your weird ass ex-girlfriend recorded during amateur night is still around. It exists, my friends. And I, for one, want to see it. Again. Uh, not for any particular reason. Just for curiosity's sake, you know?"

"Okay so that's great and everything," I tell Olly. "But why the fuck is Hannah having lunch with us?"

Hannah sits next to Olly, mostly oblivious, chomping on a potato chip. A crumb of chip sticks to her lip and when she finally looks up to address the matter at hand, it's still there. I have no idea how she makes it work but she doesn't even look weird or anything. Huh.

"Oh, um, I'm the one who told Olly the recording still exists?" Hannah says with a small shrug. "Natalie told me earlier. She said she was going to destroy it after meeting with the cheerleaders, though. She wanted to let me know it was safe and if I had any further concerns she'd be happy to meet with me to address them."

"See?" Olly says with a nod. "Now what are we going to do about this?"

"Are we supposed to do anything?" Teddy asks. "It sounds like Natalie's taking care of it. I think that's a good idea, too. How bad would it be if they wanted to become politicians in the future and a video of them dancing in a stripclub got leaked? We need to think of the girls and their future, guys."

"There you go," I say, nodding along with Teddy. "This is why we can't see it. Makes sense to me."

"Does it, though?" Olly asks. "Does it *really*, Jacksy? Because, come on, dude. Are you telling me you don't want to see Little Charlie's dance again? Tell me you don't and swear to God you're telling the truth and I'll drop this here and now."

I open my mouth to say it, to lie my goddamn ass off, and... fuck. The words won't come out. I can't do it, man. I can't lie to my bros. Or God. I don't know which one is more important in my head at the moment, but either way I can't do it.

"I *knew* it!" Olly says, laughing maniacally. "Okay, so--"

"What do you think about this, Hannah?" Sam says, waiting in the wings, focusing on the object of Olly's demise.

Not that Hannah's an object. As Teddy reminds us daily, we need to treat all women with respect. They're people with their own wants, needs, and desires, and sometimes those desires line up with ours, as is the apparent case with Olly and Hannah being oddly fucking attracted to each other. But yeah, if anyone can ruin Olly's life it's her. That's all.

"I don't really know?" Hannah says, conflicted. "On the one hand, yes. I want to see how I did and Charlotte's dance was really good. It'd be cool to watch it again and see how I could do better in the future? Just in general. I don't think I'm going to enter amateur night at the Paper Slipper again anytime soon. It was fun, though."

"And on the other hand?" Sam asks, leading the witness.

"So, alright, look," Hannah says, getting into it. "I don't know if it's ever going to happen, but I have aspirations of becoming a popular gamer girl livestreamer. I want to do it right, though. I don't want to be one of those girls who dresses in almost nothing and makes money from showing her boobs. I want to be respected and valued for my insight and knowledge about computer games. If I ever get to that level it'd be pretty bad if a video of me pole dancing half naked got leaked. So... maybe it's better if Natalie destroys it?"

"Sorry, bud," Sam says to Olly. "You're outnumbered."

"Fuck," Olly grunts. "I just had high hopes, you know?"

"If it helps, you can come watch me dance during class whenever you want?" Hannah offers, batting her lashes so fucking hard.

"It's a nice offer," Olly says, sighing. "But it's not the same, you know?"

"I can, um... I mean, like, I'm not saying we should do this *now*, but there's this place I know of that lets you rent private rooms and they have a pole to dance on and, like... if we were *dating*, um... I don't know?"

Holy fuck, bro. This girl is literally offering you a private one-on-one stripclub pole dancing experience. Obviously Olly's going to realize this and drop the recording idea, right?

I can see it in his eyes. I'm looking at him right the fuck now and--

"Look, Hannah," Olly says. "I'm *trying*, you know? Seriously, I mean it. I want to do this and I want to make it work, but I'm just not sure I'm there yet. I don't want to be an asshole by telling you I am when I'm not, so I don't think that's a good idea right now. You know? It's not you. Fuck, it's definitely not you. It's me. I'm a dick. I need to learn to not be a dick first."

"...What the actual fuck?" I ask, because I really need to know.

"I don't mind if you're a dick?" Hannah says, hopeful. "Like, a little bit, you know? Only sometimes. How much of a dick are we talking about?"

"Olly has a reputation for being a very big dick," Sam says. "Not to be confused with having one. He doesn't."

"Dude, how the fuck would you know?" Olly snaps. "And don't say it's because you've seen me naked in the locker room. Have you ever heard of showers and growers, bro? Obviously I'm a grower and, no offense, but being around a bunch of dudes in the showers doesn't exactly give me any reason to grow. So basically fuck you. That's all I have to say."

"Can we talk more about being around a bunch of naked guys in the showers, though?" Hannah asks. "This is relevant to my interests."

"Nobody kisses or whatever weird ass shit you're hoping for," I tell her. "Sorry."

"What about flirty butt slapping?"

"That happens sometimes?" Teddy says.

"Dude, Teddy, it's not flirty. It's for teambuilding. Those are teambuilding ass slaps, man," I tell him.

"Sometimes they're kind of flirty, Jacksy," Sam says. "Like, in a manly bro way. Not romantic or sexual. Just bro-ing it up, smacking each other's asses."

"Alright, look," I say to everyone here. "This isn't about what happens in the locker room showers. This is about destroying evidence that could potentially risk the futures of each and every one of the girls we mostly like and would probably sometimes call our friends."

"I know Jenny's hard to deal with but I was hoping you liked her enough to call her your friend at this point, Jacksy," Teddy says, disappointed.

"I was joking, but you're right, dude. I like the girls and they're my friends. I won't joke about that shit again. Sorry, buddy."

"Thanks, man. I appreciate it."

"Okay, *but...*" Hannah says, butting in. "What if someone were to, oh, I don't know... blur our faces on the recording? Then no one would know it was us. And I guess they'd have to disguise our voices, too. Then we could keep a copy of the video and it'd be fine, right?"

"No offense, but why the fuck are you arguing for this?" I ask her. "You just said it was a good idea to destroy the recording and now you're coming up with ways to keep it?"

"I know it could come back to bite me, but come on, dude. Having a video copy of me dancing in a stripclub? It's kind of a dream."

"Fair," I say with a begrudging nod. "*But*, knowing Natalie, she wouldn't turn a copy over to some random dude for editing purposes."

"It's a liability risk," Olly agrees. "Even I know that."

"Um, I can do video editing, though," Hannah points out. "It's kind of a hobby of mine. I started practicing because I wanted to get into livestreaming and everything, you know? I haven't started that yet, but I like to practice so I'll be ready once I do."

"How fucking perfect is that?!" Olly asks, excited all over again.

"You're assuming Natalie hasn't destroyed the evidence yet," I say. "She probably has. It's gone. I don't know why we're talking about this anymore. So, you know, if we could please--"

"She hasn't destroyed it yet," Hannah says, showing me a text on her phone. "I guess we have to decide unanimously? I don't know if I'm included. Maybe I should ask? But, um, you know, Jenny and Charlotte haven't voted yet either, so..."

We share a look. Not me and Hannah. Me and the boys. We all share a look with each other that says everything we could ever possibly need to say at a time like this.

Mainly that thing is--

"Can you leave me out of this?" Teddy asks. "I don't want to think about there being a video of my sister pole dancing at a stripclub. It's sort of weird, you know?"

"It's cool, Teddy," I say, patting him on the back. "Totally understand, man."

"Thanks, Jacksy. I appreciate it."

"I can make different videos and cut out people's dances. That's probably the best option, actually," Hannah adds. "Then I can have a copy of *my* dance but no one else's, and Jenny can have a copy of hers, and it'll be hard to separate Clarissa and Angela since they danced together, but everyone else can have their own separate copies pretty easily."

"I support that," Olly says with a nod. "And look, Teddy, even if I did happen to see Jenny's tits that one time, I won't watch a recording of her dancing on a pole even if I have the opportunity. That's how much of a bro I'm going to be to you in the future."

"I wish you'd stop bringing up the fact that my sister flashed you during Truth or Dare," Teddy says. "Besides that, what you just said is almost kind of nice?"

"As much as I was angry about it at the time, Jenny showed me at the stripclub and I'm not mad anymore,"

Hannah says to Olly. "I understand what all the fuss is about. The cheerleaders were right."

"I know, right?!" Olly says, excited. "See? Do you see now, Hannah? This is why we need to be together. I mean, not now. I'm still a dick. But later, like... I *really* want to ask you out on a date. A real date. A great date. The best date you've ever had in your entire goddamn life. I just--"

"I've, um... I don't really date much, so..." she says, making this so fucking easy for him.

Just ask her, dude. Holy shit.

"Isn't this nice, guys?" Sam says, grinning wide. "Olly and Hannah bonding over how fantastic Jenny's tits are? It's romance in the making, my friends. And I, for one, couldn't be any happier."

"When you say it like that... I'm still a dick, aren't I?" Olly says. "Fuck."

"No, it's... it's fine!" Hannah says, trying her best.

I have no idea what's going on anymore and I don't even care. I text my stepsister to see what she's thinking.

Apparently this is a mistake.

> "Yo, Baby Sis, I heard about the video. Please think about your own future or whatever and decide based on that. Maybe you want to be President one day, right? It's cool if Natalie destroys it. I won't be mad."

It takes approximately nine seconds for her to reply, but when she does:

BABY SIS

> "What if in the future I want to watch it with you? Did you like my dance? I know you said you did but if you didn't it's okay. I won't be mad. But if you liked it a lot and we watched it together maybe that'd be fun? Honestly, I don't think I want to be the President. That's a lot of work and I think I'd be happy if I could just write romance novels instead. That's also a lot of work. I didn't mean it like that. But being the President is different and hard and please don't ask me to even try campaigning. Oh, unless you want to be the President? Um, Hunter, I don't want to get too far ahead of myself but does that mean I'd be the First Lady? Because I don't think I can do that either."

There's a lot to unpack there and I feel like the President part needs addressing, but I'm solely and singularly focused on the idea of watching Baby Sis dance on a pole again, this time in private where I can show her exactly what my cock thinks of this.

Anyways, I reply with:

> "I fucking loved your dance and I fully support you if you want me to watch it again with you."

Yeah, so...

CHARLOTTE

"Aye!" Jenny says, raising her hand. "Thanks, Hannah!"

"Um, me too," I say, nervously lifting my hand a little. "Aye?"

"We have unanimous consensus then," Natalie says, sighing and shaking her head. "As ill-advised as I believe this is, I find mild comfort in the idea of Hannah editing the video herself. I'd like to be present for all video manipulation, though. Is that alright?"

"Um, sure?" Hannah says, shrugging. "We could all do it together if you want?"

"Oh, yes!" Clarissa squeals, beyond excited. "Please! Hannah, can I pick my voice? I want to make sure I sound sexy and hot and not like a man."

"Yes, totally," Angela agrees. "Hannah, is that possible?"

"Yes?" Hannah says, confused. "I can show you a couple options and see what you think?"

"Okay!"

"Oh, and can you make sure my face is blurred, but, like, pretty?" Clarissa asks.

Angela nods. "Agreed."

"I have no idea what that means but I can try?" Hannah says. "Is there anything else?"

"Um, I just want to watch mine how it was recorded," I say. "Oh, but right-side up. S-sorry!"

"Easy!" Hannah says, excited. "Jenny?"

"I'm good," Jenny says. "I'm planning to watch it on my own and relive my glory days when I'm sixty years old or something. Gonna tell my grandkids how hot I was in college."

"You totally are, too," Clarissa agrees, nodding.

"Thanks, babe!" Jenny says, giggling. "Hug?"

"Hug!"

"Group hug!" Angela calls out. "Natalie, you too. I know you hate group hugs but this one's mandatory."

"That sounds like a sexual harassment lawsuit waiting to happen, but fine," Natalie says, rolling her eyes. Despite the eyeroll, she happily joins the group hug.

I think that's it and this is the end of a fun little story that, um... I don't know what the moral of it is but maybe friendship and stuff? I think that's nice.

Except then I get a text message from Erica while we're grouphugging.

ERICA (WHY IS SHE SO MEAN?)

"I know you think you won the Stepbro Triathlon but what I didn't tell you before is the last event is WINNER TAKES ALL. You thought you'd won, didn't you? Well, you didn't! Your dance at amateur night was bad, by the way. I know I secretly recorded it and I was going to use it as blackmail against all of you, but you know what? Not even worth it. I'm glad that ugly pretend paralegal girl found out and stole my camera. I'd be embarrassed blackmailing you with your awful dances. Oh, and if you try to use my dance against me, just know that I know how hot I am and how stupidly sexy I look. Show my dance to Huntsy all you want. You know he wants to see it. Tell him he can have this whenever he wants. He's mine after the last event anyways. Anywho! This weekend. After midterms. Meet in the library. Yours. The college one. Not the public library. Don't be dumb. I'll bring everything we need and we'll see once and for all who Huntsy's TRUE STEPSISTER is. It's not you, by the way. Alright, toodles!"

"Why is she so mean?" Angela asks. "Seriously, who hurt her?"

"I think it was her stepbrother?" Clarissa says. "He seemed nice at the stripclub, though."

"He *was* nice, wasn't he?" Jenny says. "I don't get it, either."

"Why does she think Hunter's is her stepbrother, though?" I ask. "It's confusing."

"I didn't think about it before, but it really is, isn't it?" Hannah adds. "Huh."

Right, so, um...

I hope the final event isn't too hard, but I'm still going to try my best and fight for Hunter!

If I win I want to tell him I love him again after...

Oh gosh, my cheeks hurt already.

THE STEPBRO FINAL EXAM

Episode 180

CHARLOTTE

The final showdown is about to begin...

I'm not entirely sure what that means because I thought this was supposed to be a triathlon-style event? Like, um... there's three different competitions and Erica and I are supposed to go against each other in a best two-out-of-three challenge to figure out who gets to be Hunter's stepsister. I sort of understand that part, but I also really don't understand that part? I've been pretty confused this whole time and I've just kind of gone along with it because Erica seemed really insistent, but is this actually the end or is there going to be more?

Because I kind of already won, you know? I won two of the three events so far, and I thought that meant it was over, but then she said this event counts for more. Why didn't we start with this one? Then we wouldn't have had to do the other two, right? Except dancing at the stripclub was amazing and I liked it a lot and I think Hunter did also, so, um... yes...

But seriously, I think it's more up to our parents as to who is whose stepbrother or stepsister, right? To be honest, I didn't even want Hunter to be my stepbrother when I first met him. It made everything awkward. But *also,* I don't know if he would've kept talking to me if he wasn't my stepbrother? I honestly have no idea. I feel like maybe he used the stepbrother thing to tease me even more and he may have continued teasing me regardless, but it's a little too late to go back and ask him since all of that already happened.

Yes, so, um... anyways...

I'm sitting in the library, promptly on time, waiting for Erica's arrival. I'm not sure how she's going to get into the library because she doesn't go to this college. Also I was planning on having a quiet library day to myself so I could catch up on my romance story writing. Which I was doing for an hour, typing away on my laptop, until everything kind of came to a head just now.

This is how that happened:

"I'm going to step out for a bit, Charlotte," the librarian behind the front desk says to me, smiling. "You'll be fine on your own, right?"

"Um, yes," I say, nodding back, taking my new duties seriously.

I'm often the only person in the library, but when she's gone I do my best to keep everything running smoothly. Which, um... I just help people find books if they need help? It's not hard. Oh, and I show them how to use the automated check-out thing to borrow them if they want. It's pretty easy. I've done it a bunch of times already and I'm happy to assist!

The woman behind the front desk grabs her purse and heads out to do whatever needs doing. I have no idea. I feel like maybe I should ask but also I'm shy and I don't want to pry, you know? I have no idea how other people ask people questions so easily. I wish I could do that. I don't even know what I'd ask, though. That's the trouble, isn't it?

As soon as she's gone, the cheerleaders rush in, dressed in their cheer uniforms, pompoms at the ready, prepared to cheer like their lives depend on it.

"Did it start yet?!" Angela asks, blinking as she looks every which way around the library.

"Um, did it end already?" Clarissa adds, equally confused. "Nobody's here."

"Babe, that's because it didn't start yet," Angela points out.

"But what if it's because it's already over?" Clarissa counters.

They give each other equally confused looks, as if the idea of it being one or the other is obviously correct, except maybe it's both somehow? I don't know how it could be, but if anyone can figure it out, it's them.

"I'm here!" Jenny says, sashaying through the front entrance to the library, basking in the glory of all the books. "Oh, she's not here yet."

"What if it's over already, Jenny?" Clarissa ponders. "What if Erica left?"

"Did you ask Charlotte?"

The cheerleaders have a lightbulb moment, one where they've finally realized how to answer all their questions. They rush to the table I'm at, two pairs of hands holding pompoms planted on the tabletop, watching me, expectant.

"Ummmm... hi?" I mumble, blinking very fast.

"Charlie," Clarissa says, excited. "Is it already over? Did you win?"

"Or did it not start yet, babe?" Angela offers. "Do we need to, like, hype you up, because we can totally hype you up, Charlie."

"We can hype her up even if it's already over, right?" Clarissa points out.

"Babe, we *can*, but we need to know what kind of hyping up we need to do, you know?"

"Oh, right, totally."

Then Hunter shows up, followed by Sam, Teddy, and Oliver. They swagger into the library, looking like those boys in every TV show or movie ever about college guys who play football who suddenly find themselves in a library. I mean, it's really apt and on point, isn't it? Oliver slides up to the front desk and reads the cover of one of the books someone left behind that the librarian hasn't had time to reshelf yet. Teddy scans the bookcases as if he's never seen anything quite like this before. Sam looks around as if he's hoping to find someone to flirt with.

And, um... Hunter just looks straight at me, hair slightly tousled from having just gotten out of the shower after football practice. He watches me for a second, eyes smoldering, lips pursed and slightly pouty, model-like, and then he breaks into a wide grin, smiling at me like I'm everything and a little extra, like when you get french fries at a fast food restaurant but they overfill the bag and you get way more than you thought you'd get. That's, um... I'm not a bag of french fries but if I were that's the kind I'd be right now. The really good, extra kind.

"Yo," Hunter says, stepping up to the desk alongside the cheerleaders. "When's it start, Baby Sis?"

"What if it ended already, though?" Clarissa asks him.

"Uh, it didn't," he says.

"How do you know? Charlie, did you tell Hunter already? What about me~!"

"Dude, calm down," he says to Clarissa. "It didn't start because we literally just saw Erica trying to sneak into the building with Lance. It's not going well. I think she forgot she needs a student ID to get on campus."

"I think that means Charlie wins by default, right?" Sam says with a grin. "Good job!"

"Um, thanks," I say, confused. "I don't know if that's fair, though?"

"I don't know if you've realized this yet, but Erica doesn't fight fair," Olly points out. "So take the win, Little Charlie. Claim your man. Go forth and do unspeakable things to your stepbrother. Just, you know, stay safe, use protection, don't have babies or whatever, don't do anything that'll get you thrown into jail, either. Uh, what else?"

"I don't know if we should call them *unspeakable* things," Teddy points out. "That makes it sound like the things are inherently wrong, you know? But if two people have a strong connection and want to show that in an intimate and loving way, that's not wrong, is it?"

"Dude, what the fuck do you want me to call them?" Olly asks. "*Speakable* things?"

"Maybe just things?" Teddy offers.

"...Go forth and do things to your stepbrother?" Olly says, trying it out. "I mean, it doesn't have quite the same ring to it, but it mostly works. Huh. You might be onto something, buddy."

"We can work on it," Teddy says. "I'm sure there's a good word."

"What about *cuddly* things?" Angela offers. "Like, that sounds fun, right? Cuddly has lots of different uses, too. Like, you and I could be cuddly and watch a movie, Teddy. Or we could be cuddly and flirty while having a picnic in bed together. Or we could be super cute and cuddly with your, you know, cuddly wuddly cock in my cutie wootie kitty. Me~ow?"

"I think Angela's trying to come on to you, Teddy," Sam says. "She's using baby talk. That's a surefire sign a girl's into you."

"Guys, we're *just* friends," Teddy says, exasperated, sighing. "I don't know why everyone keeps--"

"Teddy! What the heck!" Jenny says, rushing over to her brother, hands on her hips, glaring at him. "Have you been cuddling with Angela? Cuddly wuddly cutie wootie? She's my *friend*, Teddy!"

"...I have no idea what you're referring to..." Teddy says, suspicious as anything.

"I think she's specifically asking if you and Angela are fucking," Hunter tells him. "But in a cuddly way? I don't fucking know, man. This entire conversation is weird as hell."

"So, like, Charlie," Clarissa says, coming back to me. "Did it end already or did it start yet? You never said."

"It, um..." I start to say, to answer the question, except then Erica shows up and I don't know if I have to anymore?

"Hey, losers!" Erica yells, strutting into the library like it's her own personal domain. "I'm finally here. You can bow down before me now."

Embarrassed, Lance hurries in after her. Behind him, Natalie clicks into the library on her high heels, her usual black pencil skirt clinging to her legs, her white blouse conservatively buttoned up almost all the way to the top. Natalie has a folder with papers tucked under her arm, cradling it like a prized possession, something incredibly valuable and important.

"Sorry," Lance says immediately after Erica does her thing. "We would've been here sooner but we didn't realize we'd need a student ID to get into the building. Natalie helped, though. Thanks, Natalie. That was really nice of you."

"You're welcome," Natalie says, sizing him up, glasses perched neatly on her nose.

"Don't *apologize* to these bimbos," Erica huffs. "Lance, seriously, this is how I know you're not my real stepbro. Do you even have any idea what you're doing? I'd offer to teach you but you don't listen. It's like you don't understand what's going on."

"You never explain anything!" Lance snaps back. "Seriously, Erica, if you just told me what you actually wanted instead of saying the weirdest, craziest stuff, I'd do my best.

But instead you joke around about, what, me breaking into your room at night? I don't even understand how that's a joke? It's not funny."

Erica stares at him for ten solid seconds before turning her full attention on me. She stomps through the library, pushing between the cheerleaders, and glares at me as I sit quietly across the table from her, my laptop still in front of me, the document for my romance story up on the screen.

"*See?*" Erica snaps, exasperated. "*This* is what I have to deal with. You don't even *understand* the pain and torment I go through every single day knowing that you have *Huntsy* and I have... *this.*" She gestures to Lance with an angry flourish. "But *not* for long. No sirree! We end this *today*, Charlotte. If that's even your real name! Ugh. I don't know what you have to hide but I'm *this* close to reporting you to the FBI. Don't even *try* me."

"I think what Erica's trying to say is she's created a simple test that I've conveniently printed out for the two of you," Natalie informs me, holding the folder in her hands now. "I'll be acting as your unbiased third-party test proctor, mediator, and final test results coordinator. We can begin as soon as you're ready. Erica's included a handy sheet of rules and stipulations and I can assure you they're decidedly fair, all things considered."

"*That*," Erica says, snatching the rules sheet from Natalie's folder. The cheerleader's legal advisor glares at her but lets her get away with it for now. "Read this and let's finally finish what we started. It won't take long. I mean, it might take *forever* for you because you won't know *any* of the answers, but I'll be done in about ten minutes. You can just give up now if you want? I know how embarrassing it is to fail a test you thought you'd ace. You definitely *won't* pass this one. Not even close. You're going *down*, girlie!"

I, um... I take the sheet of paper she's frantically waving in my face, mostly because she's waving it in my face but also because I didn't realize we were doing a test as our final challenge and I definitely didn't study for it. I've been focusing on my finals and I've done pretty well on those so far, but, um... if I knew Erica's final event was a test I would've spent some time studying for that, too.

Right, so, I read the sheet quickly and basically it's this:

It's not really a test. All the test questions are about stepbros. Stepbros *aren't* simply stepbrothers with a few less letters. Not even close! A stepbro is a mindset, a man with a desperate, passionate need to claim his stepsister in any and all ways possible. Mostly physically, but along with the body comes the heart, mind, and soul, and then there's the forbidden risk of pregnancy which is so freaking hot, and don't even get me started on having to hide everything from your parents. A stepbro and stepsister relationship is the purest form of love that can ever possibly exist and to deny that is to deny human nature.

I want to add quick that this is what Erica wrote and I don't know if I agree with it but she has very strong opinions on the subject.

Right, um, and on to the rules...

- 1 - We have ten minutes to finish answering five questions.

- 2 - Some of the questions are multiple choice but some are essays. For the multiple choice questions, you aren't allowed to guess. You have to explain your answer after if asked to.

- 3 - For the sake of fairness, we'll defer to the stepbros in question on the answers. *(Mainly Huntsy but I guess Lance can help, ugh.)*

- 4 - All questions are stepbro-related or -adjacent. If you know, you know. If you don't, too bad, sucker.

- 5 - Seriously, if you don't know, you've already failed, and just admit it before we start so I don't have to waste my time. K THANKS.

I raise my hand after reading the rules to, um, ask about... I really *don't* know, so...

"Don't," Natalie says, glaring at me. "I know what you're about to do and I'm telling you right now that you won't be doing it, Charlotte."

"Oh, okay," I say, lowering my hand. "S-sorry!"

"It's fine. I'm simply keeping your best interests in mind," she offers with a faint smile.

"Can we get this over with already?" Erica snaps, shoving her butt into a chair and twirling her hair around in her fingertips until it gets curly for a second before falling straight as soon as she lets it loose.

"Um, sure," I say with a nod. "Just let me put my laptop away quick."

I do that and I fetch a pen from my bookbag, finding a second one to give to Erica. She huffs and puffs at me but takes it nonetheless. Hunter and the boys and Lance and the cheerleaders and Jenny wait in the wings as Natalie hands out the question sheets. There's two total, three questions on one page and two on the other. Oh, and a spot for our names and the date. I fill that out quick while Erica does the same.

Natalie takes out her phone, sets a timer, shows it to us, and says:

"Let the testing commence."

...I read through the questions and they're all very strange but I answer as best I can...

I hope I do alright.

HUNTER

Fuck yeah, it's my time to shine!

If all the answers rely on me saying what I think is correct, I can basically give it all to Baby Sis, no questions asked. Right? Even if Erica gets one right, I can just lie and say she's wrong. Who's going to know the difference?

That's the plan, but in the end I don't even have to do any of that.

What the fuck kind of test is this?

Once the girls are finished writing and answering the questions, Natalie collects their sheets and takes a seat at a table nearby. She puts the two tests next to each other, side by side, and looks at us, poignant and professional.

"I'll now grade these tests to the best of my abilities," Natalie informs the group. "First, I'll read the questions out loud. Then I'll read the possible answers. As the two resident stepbrothers at hand, Hunter and Lance, if you could then formulate a shared opinion on which answer is most correct, we'll go from there. Are we ready?"

"I'm ready, *but*," Erica says, interrupting. "The questions are about *true* stepbrothers. So Huntsy's answer is more important. I wanted to point that out so you understand how you should be grading us."

"Understood," Natalie says with a nod. "Does anyone else have any other comments or concerns?"

"Do we need another stepbrother for tiebreakers?" Clarissa asks. "What if it's a tie? How does that work?"

"Judging from a cursory glance at the test sheets, I highly doubt we'll have a tie, but in the event we need a tiebreaker we can call on one of the other boys to assist. Teddy seems like our best candidate. Are you alright with that, Teddy?"

"I guess so?" Teddy says, confused. "I've never been a stepbrother, though."

"Teddy, shhh," Jenny says, shoving her hand against his mouth. "Do it for Charlotte!"

"I'm not her stepbrother either!" Teddy points out, or at least he tries to but he has Jenny's hand shoved against his mouth so it mostly comes out muffled even if I get what he's saying.

Anyways--

"First question," Natalie says, ignoring the noise. "What is Hunter Jackson's favorite pet nickname?"

"Uhhhhhh?" I grunt, because seriously what the fuck? This is a question?

"Huntsy, obviously," Erica says, answering out loud.

"That's the answer she wrote down, yes," Natalie says. "Charlotte answered that she doesn't think Hunter wants her to call him by a pet nickname, but he likes when his friends call him Jacksy."

"I didn't know if that counted?" Baby Sis says. "I think a pet nickname is, like... for boyfriends and girlfriends? So, um... yes. That's it."

"Charlotte," I say. "This one's easy. She wins."

"*What!*" Erica huffs. "Don't lie to me, Huntsy! I know how much you love being called Huntsy, Huntsy!"

"Uh, I don't, though?" I point out.

"Lance, do you have an opinion?" Natalie asks, for the sake of fairness even though all of this is bullshit.

"Not really," Lance says with a shrug. "I don't know Hunter well enough to know what he likes being called."

"Tiebreaker!" Erica demands. "I demand a recount! This shall not stand!"

"That's not how tiebreakers work, but alright," Natalie says, turning to Teddy. "Teddy, can you give us a definitive answer, once and for all, so we can move on?"

"Baby Charlie never calls Hunter Huntsy or Jacksy," Teddy says, considering the options fully and with serious commitment. "I'm pretty much positive he doesn't like being called Huntsy, though. If he *did* like being called anything, I would think it's Jacksy. So... I'm going with that. Jacksy. That's my final answer."

"This also isn't that kind of test and this isn't a game show, but thank you, Teddy," Natalie says. She takes a red pen she was hiding somewhere in her tied up, dark black hair, and marks the tests accordingly.

Erica gets a big fat **X** for question number one. Baby Sis gets a circle. Fuck yeah!

"Moving on to question number two," Natalie says, going right for it. "This is a multiple choice question. I'll read all the possible answers out loud after reading the question and we'll proceed from there."

Got it. I'm ready for this. Let's fucking go, boys.

"If a true stepbro happens to find his stepsister stuck in an awkward position that would make it easy for him to have his way with her whether she liked it or not, and even when she started protesting he kept going, and eventually she started passionately moaning about how much she loves his cock deep inside her, what should he do?" Natalie says, apparently reading this word for fucking word.

"Is that a real question?" I ask, completely stumped.

"Yes," Natalie says with a curt nod. "The options are as follows. A, he claims her fully and completely and fucks her senseless until she falls madly in love with him. B, he politely assists her in getting unstuck from whatever it is she's stuck in and then leaves without further incident. C, he gets stuck with her and they both wait for someone else to come and help them. Or, D, he ignores her completely because it's not his problem."

"This one's hard," Lance says, standing there with me, nodding thoughtfully as he listens. "Huh."

"I mean, dude, it's not *that* hard, is it?" I say.

"Since this is multiple choice, I'll wait until you two have a decision on the answer before reading Erica and

Charlotte's answers aloud," Natalie adds. "Take your time, gentleman."

"Okay, so, it's clearly not A, right?" I say, just so I know Lance and I are on the same page.

"Are we answering what we think Erica thinks the answer is?" he asks. "Or what we think it is?"

"Dude, it's what *we* think it is. Not her. That's the point. This is about us. We're the stepbros. Fuck, I didn't mean to say that. *Stepbrothers.* That's us. It's what *we* would do, so..."

Also, fuck, this one *is* kind of hard because, alright, look. If I somehow happened upon Baby Sis stuck in an awkward position where I could have my way with her... I'd consider it? I mean, I'd ask her first. But if she was *actually* in trouble and stuck, obviously I'd help her. I wouldn't ignore her, though. I don't know why the fuck anyone would get stuck with someone else and wait for others to come by and help them, either? That's weird as hell, man.

Anyways, I have an answer, because none of the multiple choice options fully fit what I'd actually do in that situation, so...

"It's not D, right?" Lance adds, helping. "Even if it's Erica, I couldn't just ignore her."

"I'd probably ignore her, but I get what you mean," I tell him. "We can cross D off the list."

"Erica would probably joke about A, but I wouldn't do that, either," Lance says with a nod.

"Same," I agree. "I think the obvious answer is B, you know? Like, why would someone get stuck with their stepsister on purpose and wait for someone else to help them instead of helping her himself? Makes no sense."

"What if it's a trick question?" Lance asks. "What if C's the answer?"

"No," I say to him. "It's not. How? How could it ever be a trick question?"

"I don't know, but I think I might pick C," Lance says with

a shrug. When I glare at him so fucking hard, he continues with, "Hear me out, Hunter! What if she's stuck in a well, you know? Like an old well at a farm and you find her there and she's crying and you're like, wait, how'd you get stuck in that well? But she doesn't know how it happened, and she's scared, right? So you call for help *first* and then you climb down the well to keep her safe and show her that everything's going to be fine while you wait for help to show up? That's why I think it could be C."

"Look, you're really fucking reaching with that one," I tell him. "But also what if you *didn't* do that and just, I don't fucking know... helped her get out of the goddamn well instead of getting stuck down there with her? Wouldn't that be better?"

"I mean, probably, but what if you need more people to lift her up? I'm not sure I could help anyone out of a well on my own, you know?"

"We're getting a little too stuck on one specific example," I say. "I think we're supposed to think more in generalities."

"Oh, you think?" Lance says, brow furrowed. To Natalie, he asks, "Can we get an example of a situation the stepsister in question might get stuck?"

"I believe you're overthinking this question, but yes, I'll allow that," she says. "Erica? Charlotte? Examples, please."

"A washing machine, obviously," Erica instantly says. "Maybe in a yoga pose, too? Oh! Or if I got my head stuck in a railing while going up some stairs. Like my head's in between the wooden bars, you know?"

"Ummm... the only thing I can think of is, um..." Baby Sis says, stumbling. "If I locked myself in the art club storage closet maybe? Is that okay?"

"Yes, that's fine," Natalie says, smiling to her. "Boys? Your answer, please."

"B," we both easily say at the same time.

"It is *not*," Erica fumes. "It's absolutely one-hundred percent A and you *know* it, Huntsy!"

"Please refrain from harassing the judges," Natalie says, shaking her head. "If this continues, I'll need to ask you to leave."

Erica gets a big red **X** again and Charlotte gets an **O**. Fuck yeah!

Question number three is tricky, though...

"If you fell in love with your stepbro and did all sorts of dirty, raunchy, rude, nasty, naughty, sexy, hot, steamy, spicy things with him, and you were happy with that, what would you tell your parents?" Natalie asks. "Again, this is multiple choice. A, nothing, you'd keep it a secret for as long as possible. B, you'd immediately tell your parents you're madly in love with your stepbro and you don't care if they approve or not. Or, C, you'd talk to your parents and try to get them to understand the situation but if they didn't agree you'd break up."

"Fuck," I grunt. "Uh..."

"What if none of that happens?" Lance asks. "I don't understand the question."

"*If*," Erica screeches at him. "The question is *if* it happens, Lance. My God! Use your stupid brain!"

"Sorry, but these questions are really confusing and honestly more than a little strange, Erica!"

Baby Sis stares at me from under her lashes, nervously looking down at the table as if she knows she probably got this one wrong. At least if she answered the question the way we've been doing things, she did. That's on me, though. I'm the one who asked her if we could wait, if we could figure stuff out before telling our parents.

It's fucking hard, you know? Like, not only do we have to tell my dad and her mom, but we have to tell *her* dad and *my* mom, too. Why the fuck are they both married and what did we ever do to deserve this?

What if none of them approve? What if, like... one out of four approves? What if it's a fifty-fifty split? I have no fucking clue, man. It's all way too confusing and I fully realize we probably should've talked about this at some point, but we *haven't*, so...

"What are you thinking?" Lance asks, nose scrunched up. "I honestly have no idea, man. Sorry."

I know the answer I should go with but for the life of me I don't know if I can say it out loud right now...

DIRTY LITTLE NO GOOD LYING CHEATER!

Episode 181

CHARLOTTE

I f you fell in love with your stepbrother and did all sorts of stuff with him, and you were happy with that, what would you tell your parents?

That's the third question on Erica's test and I really struggled with my answer even though it's multiple choice. I think I struggled with it so much *because* it's multiple choice.

And, um, you know...

- A.) Nothing, you'd keep it a secret for as long as possible.

- B.) You'd immediately tell them you were madly in love with your stepbrother and you don't care if they approve or not.

or

- C.) You'd talk to them and try to get them to understand the situation but if they didn't agree you'd break up.

I feel like none of those answers encompasses any of what Hunter and I are doing. I don't even think any of them fits what I would want to do now. This should definitely be an essay question with more nuance and context, but that's not an option on this test. I wonder what the right answer is, or at least what one Erica thinks is right? I wonder what choice Hunter's going to pick, too.

We, um... we've kept it a secret so far? For as long as possible? I don't really know. We've kind of vaguely hinted at the idea that we're going to talk to our parents about it at some point but we haven't set up any specific plans for it, so...

We definitely didn't immediately tell them. Oh gosh, how embarrassing would that have been? Like, um... after Hunter and I had sex for the first time in his bedroom at his mom's place and... the next morning when my dad and his mom were downstairs, very shortly after we found out they were now married?

I can just imagine how *that* would've gone.

"Hey, um, dad, hi, I want you to know I really like Hunter and we're going to be dating now. We just decided it this morning after he took my virginity last night. And, um, know this is kind of sudden but you sprang your new marriage on me too, so... okay that's it, that's all I wanted to say."

Nope...

I feel like the last option fits best, or at least the first part does. Hunter and I need to talk to our parents and hope they understand.

But what if they don't?

I have no idea. I don't want to break up with him, but what are we supposed to do if both of our parents seriously dislike the fact that we're dating? Um, I don't know if my mom will be that upset, but she might be kind of upset? She likes

Hunter, but I think she likes him as her stepson and not as my boyfriend. I don't know who she wants to be my boyfriend, if she ever got to pick, but she's been pretty into the idea of it being Sam, at least earlier on when she thought he was asking me on a fake date with plans on turning it into something real.

Oh, and she's been excited about Teddy too. We aren't even dating and I'm really confused about why she thought we were even if we *did* pretend to be a couple at the vegan Mexican restaurant. I guess if Hunter and I are going to tell our parents we're dating, we also need to tell them who we aren't dating, and that's, um...

What the heck am I doing with my life...

Anyways! Yes! Umm!

I answer as best I can and I hope I did alright but I really have no idea. Hunter and Lance are trying to decide what they think is the best answer right now, too. They're taking a whole lot of time. Erica sits across from me at my table in the library, this smug, super satisfied look on her face, like she knows she's got this one in the bag and even if she's been wrong on the first two questions, well... this is when she makes her big comeback!

I don't know how the scoring system works for this test idea she came up with, either. Is it the person who scores the highest? That makes sense, but maybe the questions are weighted differently and essay questions count for more points, which, um... that *also* makes sense?

I'm so confused.

"Alright, look, I think I know the answer," Hunter says, announcing this to Natalie. "I also want to preface by saying this *isn't* what I've personally done in the past, and I don't know if that's, uh... you know, hypocritical? But that's not what the question is and, come on, let's be real fucking honest here, the question's kind of fucked up, isn't it?"

"Are you finished?" Natalie asks, smirking. "This isn't an

exam critique, Hunter. You can just give the answer. Whenever you're ready then?"

"Uh, B," he says. "The answer is B."

Erica's face goes pale and she frantically looks around the library for... something. I have no idea what. When she sees me looking at her, she makes a face and sticks her tongue out.

"If that's the consensus, then--" Natalie starts to say.

Lance clears his throat and interrupts her. "Actually, I was going to go with Hunter's answer, but I think maybe it's A instead?"

"A? Are you for real, dude? How is it A?" Hunter asks, taken aback.

"The answers are too hard!" Lance says. "Dude, are you seriously saying you'd tell your parents and you don't care what they think? I care what my parents think."

"So... that sounds like a C to me..." Hunter points out. "Not that that's the answer, either. It's not. But you literally just said A but now you sound like you mean C?"

"I thought about it, but if I were in love then I don't know if I could break up with someone that easily, you know?"

Hunter pauses and stares at him and it takes awhile but eventually he begrudgingly nods.

"I fully respect that, man," my stepbrother says. "I get you."

"Right, so, look, I'm not saying any of the answers are good. But if I *had* to pick one, I think I'd go with A, you know? That's all I meant."

"Are we going with A then?" Natalie asks.

Erica perks up, face no longer flush, ready and waiting to score a massive victory against all odds.

"Sorry, but I'm sticking with B," Hunter says. Erica's manic grin falls flat again.

"I'm going with A," Lance adds.

"Teddy?" Natalie says, calling Jenny's brother to the stand. "Your informed tiebreaker decision, please?"

Teddy nervously stands up from his chair while everyone watches him. Jenny's especially invigorated right now, basically shouting under her breath for Teddy to just pick B. Pick it, Teddy! Do it for Charlotte!"

"Okay, I listened to everything Jacksy and Lance just said, and I thought about it a lot myself," Teddy says. "I don't have any experience with this kind of question, so I don't know if it's fair for me to answer, though? But. Jenny, I'm doing it! Stop yelling at me!" he adds as soon as Jenny starts to boo. "I think I'd go with C? I'm not saying I'd *want* to break up, but I really like my parents, guys. And the thing is, if I were in a situation like that, I think they'd understand? The answer specifically mentioned if they *didn't* understand, right? But if they did, we wouldn't have to break up. I think I'd be able to convince them and I think they'd accept my relationship."

"I feel the need to point out that generally in the event of a tiebreaker situation you're supposed to actually break the tie instead of continuing it," Natalie says, serious and stern.

"Actually, I change my answer to C, too," Hunter says. "I hadn't thought about it the way Teddy did but he makes a valid point."

"He really does," Lance says, now in full agreement. "I'm going with C, too."

"Aw, thanks!" Teddy says, smiling wide at the two of them. "That means a lot. I know you guys give me shit sometimes for maybe being a little, I don't know what the word is, but I don't always catch on as fast, you know? So it means a lot to me when I try my best for you guys and you recognize that."

"Bro, of course," Hunter says, teary-eyed. "I know we fuck with you sometimes, but you're one of my best bros, Teddy. Love you, man. Don't ever think otherwise, okay?"

"I don't know you that well but I think you're cool, Teddy," Lance adds. "That was some great insight, man."

The three boys enjoy their bonding moment and, um... I don't have the heart to tell them, but thankfully Natalie does.

"Unfortunately neither Charlotte nor Erica chose C," Natalie informs the crowd. "Erica picked A and Charlotte picked B. Moving on to the next question--"

"What!" Hunter cries out, staring at his ex. "*You* picked A? What the actual fuck?"

"That's the *fun* part, Huntsy!" Erica whines. "How do you not understand that? Why would I want to tell our parents when we could keep sneaking around and being hot and forbidden for as long as possible? I can't even with this. You're so silly. Seriously, I'll teach you everything you need to know if we can just stop this stupid charade and run away together."

"Uh, yeah, no thanks," he says, rolling his eyes.

"I, um... I picked B but I didn't mean it like that?" I say to him, just in case he thinks I'm wrong, too. "I... I m-meant, um... I would fight for you, Hunter! I actually think I should've maybe picked C now but also I don't think I would want to break up with you if our parents don't understand? I still think maybe B is good but this test is honestly really hard."

"Nah, it's cool," Hunter says, grinning back. "You're doing great, Baby Sis."

"...Thanks," I mumble, blushing.

We still have two more questions to go, though.

"Next up is another essay question," Natalie informs the stepbrothers. "If you could plan a perfect day with your stepbro, what would it involve? Please describe it in extremely specific detail, starting with waking up in the morning and all the way through the day until going to sleep at night." She pauses for a second, before adding, "I'll now read the answers out loud, starting with Erica's, and let you choose whichever you think is best."

"Please don't," Hunter says as Natalie clears her throat.

"My answer is *clearly* superior," Erica says right as Natalie starts.

And, um... oh wow, what the...

I kind of blank out partway through but it's basically this, except not censored:

"We wake up with Huntsy's **<censored>** already deep inside my tight hot wet **<censored>** and we **<censor>** until we can't **<censor>** anymore because we're starving, so we shower except then we get our second wind and **<censor>** **<censor>** **<censored>** before heading down for breakfast to **<censor>** **<censor>** with a croissant and **<censored>** on the **<censor>** while our parents **<censor>** in the **<censored>** **<censor>**. Afterwards we **<censor>** in the **<censored>** while we **<censor>** our **<censors>** and--"

This continues for approximately five minutes before Natalie finishes. She has to turn the page a quarter of the way through to read everything that's written on the back, too. It's a lot.

"Charlotte wins this round," Hunter says once she's done.

"I know we need to be unbiased but I don't think I would ever go with that answer?" Lance adds, mostly in agreement.

"I understand where you're coming from but for the sake of fairness I need to read Charlotte's answer, too," Natalie adds.

The boys nod and I nod and the cheerleaders look slightly confused but they also nod. Teddy doesn't nod, he just looks mildly horrified. Right, so, um...

My answer was just that we'd wake up and have a really nice breakfast that we'd make together. We'd have eggs and bacon and toast. Then we'd go for a walk in the park and buy ice cream and after that we'd check out a thrift shop and do a thrift shop date where we picked out cute clothes for each other because I liked it when Hunter and I did that before.

Then maybe I would need a little break? But Hunter could

stay with me and we could write more of our stories. I like his and I hope he keeps writing it so I can read it. I like that he reads mine and helps me with it, too.

I forgot about lunch but sometimes I forget about lunch so that's fine. Then we'd get pizza and loaded waffle fries at the pizza place we like to go to, and we'd watch a movie and cuddle in bed and maybe things would get steamy at that point like in a romance novel or maybe they would have earlier, but I just kind of like to let stuff like that happen naturally and if we didn't do it at all I'd still be really happy.

Oh, and I want to fall asleep cuddled up next to him in his arms and I hope I wake up like that, too.

"What pizza place has loaded waffle fries?" Lance asks, eyes wide, staring at Hunter.

"Dude, I'll totally show you the spot!" Hunter says, excited. "It's this easy to miss place nearby. The old man who owns it is chill. Really nice guy. The pizza's great but the loaded waffle fries are fucking fantastic. For real. Baby Sis always gets extra fried jalapenos with it and they're really good but I don't know how she handles all that heat. I can only eat a few before I need to stop, but she goes hard and just destroys them all. It's amazing."

"That sounds great," Lance says, then adds, "I'm going with Charlotte's answer."

"Same," Hunter says. "Easiest choice ever."

"*How?!*" Erica frets. "How are waffle fries better than **<censored>**! In what world does that *ever* make sense?!"

"They really are great, though," Clarissa says, reluctant to admit it. "I don't know if they're better than sex *all* the time, but they're better than a lot of the sex I've had?"

"Totally, babe," Angela says. "Like, good sex is the best, but sometimes it's bad and then I could totally go for some of Charlie's loaded waffle fries instead."

"We just can't eat them that often because they have a lot

of carbs, but I love when we sneak some in with Charlie. Love you, Charlie!"

"Love you too, Clarissa!" I say back, excited. I'm glad everyone loves loaded waffle fries as much as I do.

"So..." Jenny says, slow and ready. "Charlotte's already correctly answered three out of five of the questions. That means she wins, right?"

"No!" Erica says, interrupting before Natalie can confirm. "The last question is the *most* important. It counts double. Whoever answers that one correctly wins."

"I've just been informed that the last question counts twice," Natalie says, as if she didn't just hear Erica say it. "Which still means Charlotte has a higher score than Erica, as Erica's answered absolutely nothing correctly so far and Charlotte's already answered three questions correctly. But, for my own amusement, because I'm very much intrigued by this question, let's continue, shall we?"

"Okay," I say, nodding, fully prepared.

"I meant it counts for four points," Erica says quick. "Sorry, I'm distracted by how hot Huntsy looks today."

"Uh, okay?" Hunter says, furrowing his brow. "I look the same as I do every day?"

"Your hair's a little different?" I point out. "It's, um... I think it's because you took a shower after practice? I like it a lot, too."

"Yeah?" Hunter says, grinning and winking at me. "How much do you like it, Baby Sis?"

"Shhhhhhh, I'm busy, Hunter! Don't flirt with me right now please. I'm too nervous."

He laughs and rolls his eyes and everyone smiles except for Erica, who huffs and glares at me.

"The final question..." Natalie says, pausing for effect. "For *four* points, which will make one of you our clear winner, multiple choice again, the last question is..."

I swallow hard and wait for her to say it out loud even

though I already know what it is. I took the test, but, um... this is all very dramatic and I feel like I'm in a reality TV show now but it's a really strange one about stepbrothers? Yup. Okay, um...

"What is Hunter Jackson's favorite movie genre?" Natalie asks, reading the question. "The choices are as follows. A, sci-fi movies about aliens that no one even understands. B, hot and heavy hardcore porn. C, boring documentaries. Or D, this is the wrong answer but if you think it's something else write it down here and enjoy failing hard, loser."

"I was trying to follow along but could you read the answers again?" Hunter asks, staring at her. "I feel like I heard them wrong."

"I got confused, too," Lance adds. "I thought they'd be phrased more like, you know... romance movies, or fantasy movies, or whatever?"

"Yeah..."

Natalie clears her throat and repeats herself to the satisfaction of the boys.

"What are you thinking, man?" Hunter asks Lance. "It's not boring documentaries, obviously."

"I know we're supposed to come to a consensus but the question was about what movies *you* like, right?" Lance points out. "I don't actually know what you like. I've never watched a movie with you. I don't think we've talked about it, either?"

"Shit, you're right," Hunter says. "Uh... I mean, I know the answer but can we hear what answers they gave?" he asks Natalie.

"Since one of them is a write-in, that seems acceptable," Natalie says with a nod, approving his request.

"Nobody wrote anything in!" Erica screeches. "That was a *test*. A *bad* test. If Charlotte wrote something in on the answer that *literally* says you fail if you write anything in that means she--"

"Erica chose B, the hardcore porn option," Natalie says, ignoring her and answering Hunter. "Charlotte chose D with a write-in answer of bad horror movies with terrible titles."

"...What an *idiot!*" Erica screeches. "Thanks for that, though! This means I won and I'll be taking my true stepbro, Huntsy, now! Huntsy, don't worry, baby! I'll teach you everything you need to know about--"

"Definitely D," Hunter says, talking over his ex-girlfriend. "Uh, legitimately with the write-in answer Baby Sis chose. Fuck, I love super cheesy horror movies. Dude, Baby Sis, can we have a horror movie night again soon?"

"Okay!" I say, excited for both the horror movie night and also I got four extra points on the test. Yay, me. "That sounds fun."

"...What?" Erica says, staring at everyone in the library as if we're clearly insane and nobody here understands anything, least of all her vast and immense stepbro brilliance.

"Why the fuck would my favorite movie genre be hardcore porn?" Hunter asks, glaring at her.

Erica blinks, confused about the question.

"It's true," Clarissa adds. "I mean, don't get me wrong, it's fun to watch sometimes, but it's not family friendly, you know?"

"I never thought about it like that, but it makes sense, doesn't it?" Angela adds. "You want to share your favorite movies with other people so they need to be, like, totally approachable or whatever."

"Maybe not *totally* approachable," Jenny adds. "I wouldn't watch horror movies with my little cousin, you know?"

"I watched a movie about dolls with my little cousin once but I didn't realize it was about *scary* dolls and my aunt didn't let me babysit again for a year," Clarissa adds, nodding along, agreeing with Jenny. "I totally thought the dolls would be cute, you know? How was I supposed to know?"

"Was it Dollhouse Massacre Five?" Olly asks.

"That's it! That's the one!"

"Fuck, that one almost got me, too! I know the title is super on the nose, but the doll on the cover of the DVD isn't that scary looking, you know?"

"Totally," Clarissa says with a sincere nod.

"Right, so, before everyone gets carried away and talks about *that* for the next thirty minutes," Natalie says, shuffling our tests into her folder. "After tallying the scores, Charlotte is the clear winner with a score of seven against Erica's score of absolutely nothing."

"She cheated!" Erica shouts, standing hard from her chair and pointing an accusing finger at me. "You dirty little no good lying cheater! How'd you do it? Fess up right now so Huntsy knows what an awful wretched person you are!"

"I... I don't even know how to cheat on a test like this?" I answer, truthful. "Ummm... some of the questions were really hard to answer, though?"

"I *know* you cheated," Erica says, louder and louder with every word. "How do you get a score of *seven* on a *five* question test! That's impossible!"

"...You said the last question counted for four points..." I mumble.

"I did no such thing!" Erica huffs. "I demand a retest! Let's take it again! Same questions, same stepbrothers, but no cheating this time!"

"I'm pretty sure that would actually be cheating, seeing as you both know all the answers now," Natalie says, a flat refusal. "Somehow I'm positive you'd still get a lower score, though. Hmm."

"This is *ridiculous!*" Erica shrieks. "Absolutely *absurd!* How can someone like *her* beat *me* in a *stepbro* challenge. I'm literally the embodiment of *the perfect stepsis*. I don't know how anyone could think otherwise. It's *obvious*. It's so stupidly comically obvious that I can't even--"

The librarian returns from her break halfway through

Erica's extremely high-pitched rant. I wince as soon as I see her because this is definitely still a library and we're supposed to be quiet. I was in charge and I let Erica break the one main rule. I should've been more vigilant.

"Charlotte," the librarian says to me as she takes a seat behind her desk. "As nice as it is to see you and your friends enjoying yourselves, we still need to be quiet in the library."

"S-sorry!" I squeak. "Um, she's... she's very upset, that's all."

"*Upset!*" Erica rages. "I'm *furious.* I *hate* you, you stupid dirty *liar,* you disgusting *cheater,* you ignorant excuse for a *fake stepsister.* I absolutely *loathe* you and everything you stand for, you--"

"Well, that's enough of that!" the librarian lady says, reaching for the landline phone receiver on her desk. She presses some buttons and starts talking to someone on the other end. "Yes. Yes. As you can hear, there's a young lady causing a disturbance in the library. Yes. Could you? I've asked her to keep it down, but she refuses. Yes. I'll ask her to leave, but if you could send someone over just in case? Yes. Yes. Thank you!"

Then she hangs up. Erica stares at her like she can't believe that just happened. To be fair, I don't think it's ever happened before? I'm in the library a lot and usually I'm the only one here so I'd probably know if it had, at least.

"I think maybe we should leave?" Lance says to Erica. "We're bothering everyone, Erica. We don't even go to this college, so..."

"I think that's a very good idea," the librarian says to him, arms crossed over her chest, stern.

"This isn't the end!" Erica shouts, one last hurrah before getting kicked out of the library. "You haven't seen the last of me, Charlotte! If that's even your real name! Ha! I'll be back! I'll take what's rightfully mine and claim Huntsy as my one true stepbro! Just you wait!"

"Alright, Erica. That's enough," Lance says, ushering her out into the hall. "Sorry!" he says to the librarian on the way out. "She, uh... yeah, she gets like this and that's not an excuse or anything, but I'm really very sorry. It won't happen again."

"Thank you," the librarian says to him. "You're welcome back anytime if you can keep to the rules. She's not, though. Bye bye!"

She waves as they leave and everything.

"Dude," Hunter says to me after they're gone. "You won. You won every challenge. You won the Stepbro Triathlon!"

Natalie nods, confirming my first place position. The cheerleaders squeal and start to do a quickie version of a cheer right in the middle of the library. Sam and Olly and Teddy talk to Jenny about how maybe it was a little touch and go at the end for a second, but everything worked out for the best.

And I, um...

"*Shhhhhhh!*" I say, hushing everyone. "This is a library. Please. We need to be quiet."

They quiet down immediately. The cheerleaders freeze mid-cheer which looks funny but they're quiet and that's what's important right now.

The librarian gives me a smile and a thumbs up from behind her desk.

I sit quietly in my chair again and open my laptop back up and, um...

I pat the chair next to me nervously and look over at Hunter. "Do you, um... d-do you want to read what I wrote today?"

"Yeah," he says, sitting down, kissing me on the cheek. "Let's see it, Baby Sis."

Yay, I won.

I fought for you, Hunter!

PLOT TWIST

Episode 182

A STORY FROM CHARLOTTE SCOTT'S PRIVATE LAPTOP

---

*(**Characters** - Chantel Scout, Huntley Jacobs, and the Mystery Murderer!)*

*(**Setting** - Chantel and Huntley running through the woods, trying to evade the mysterious man who broke into her rented log cabin in the middle of the night...)*

"Shit," Huntley mutters under his breath, scanning the dark woods. "We need to get out of here."

He didn't have to tell her twice. Chantel knew full well the situation they were in. It was something out of a movie or a dream or maybe both, but definitely not the kind of scenario anyone expected to happen in real life. Least of all after she and Huntley had just... in her bed... multiple times over, to her immense satisfaction...

Snap out of it, Chantel! Now was *not* the time to be daydreaming about that thing Huntley did with his tongue earlier. Seriously, though. Where'd he learn a trick like that?

"This way," Huntley says, grabbing her hand and pulling her through the woods. "We'll head to my cabin for now. Should be safe there. I'll call the sheriff once we're inside."

"What about--" she started to say, but as fast as the words began to form they were useless.

The mysterious man who'd broken into her cabin, cutting the power before shattering one of the glass panes in the door so he could unlock it and let himself in, well... he was right behind them, the shadow of his silhouette visible in the dim light of the half moon resting high in the sky. The forest's canopy overhead gave them cover, but the moon's gentle light sliced through the scattering of leaves, leaving puddles of light on the forest floor near their feet.

It was a midnight game of hide and seek, except in this case the man who was *it* was out for blood.

Chantel started to scream as soon as she saw the hooded figure, instinctive if not logical. Maybe he hadn't seen them? Maybe he didn't know where they were? If she stayed quiet, they could hide, make it to Huntley's cabin, and--

Her sharp scream cut through the woodsy cricket's lullabye, slicing through the forest song and wind and rustle of leaves. For a fraction of a second, her scream was the only sound anyone within a mile could've heard, and then, just as soon as she started, Huntley clapped his hand over her mouth.

He pulled her behind a tree, their feet kicking up a dry, dirty pile of leaves. The man chasing them had definitely heard her, but whether he realized where the scream came from was still up for debate.

"Dammit!" Huntley grunted, a harsh whisper. "Look, I'm not mad at you, but--"

The shadowy figure ran past them, right beside them, barely a few feet away. She could reach out and touch him from here, could see the sharpened blade held tight in his hand as he searched for them in the woods. Long, silver, glistening, she recognized the chef's knife from her cabin, the one they'd used to make regular, everyday meals multiple times over.

If this man had his way, soon it would be used to make quick work of them instead.

Huntley froze, pulling her tight against his body. The leaves beneath their feet crinkled like Christmas wrapping paper, crushed and torn by the tread of their shoes. Their assailant nearly kept going. Nearly. But at the last second something beckoned to him, a sound or intuition, something he saw out of the corner of his eye.

He stopped dead, turned, and spotted them huddled behind the tree, lambs for the slaughter.

"Run!" Huntley shouted, bellowing the word like a bear protecting his cubs.

Chantel flung herself away from the tree just in time, evading the knife that came crashing against the bark where she'd just been. She screamed again. Huntley didn't try to stop her this time. No point, she supposed. No reason to try and--

They hadn't been able to dress for the woods, for the night, for the weather, before fleeing from her rented cabin. They'd just finished making love, fucking, raw and intimate, passionate and real, when this wayward intruder had interrupted them. Huntley wrenched on whatever clothes he could to drag on in record time; his pants and shirt laying by her bed. Chantel wasn't as lucky. She somehow found a suitable pair of shoes, but her only readily available clothes were the ones she'd worn to seduce the hunky lumberjack in the first place.

Yes, she was running through the woods in her panties, bra, and a black silk negligee; the same one she'd worn Huntley had barged in on her when she didn't have any clean laundry that first day.

She had shoes, though. Sort of. It was a pair of old Crocs she kept under her bed in case of an emergency. An old habit from her college days when you never knew if there'd be a fire drill in the middle of the night, real or otherwise. They were easy to put on, comfortable, and perfect in a pinch.

Usually they were fine for quick trips, but she found them incredibly lacking while on the run from a potential serial killer in the forest.

Still, she worked with what she had and this was it. She belatedly realized she'd also flung her phone into the thin pocket of her negligee. As they ran, she reached for it, fumbling around, trying to unlock it to see if she could dial someone, anyone, that could help them. No sooner than she started, her phone fell from her hands, crashing onto a crisp, crunchy pile of leaves.

Huntley surged on, strong, relentless, his body working hard to keep them safe. Chantel tried. She tried as hard as she could and adrenaline kept her going for longer than she ever thought possible, but then--

Her ill-suited footwear caught on the root of a tree and she stumbled to the ground. She tried to stand, Huntley holding her hand, pulling, trying to help, but in her fall she'd scraped her knee bad. And, from the way it felt, her ankle was in poor shape, too.

"Huntley!" Chantel cried. "I... I can't! I'm sorry! Go on without me!"

He stared at her for a second and she stared back. What was that look in his eyes? She could see something there, dark and bright, a reflection from the stray droplets of moonlight scattering through the leafy canopy coloring his eyes, iridescent, a glimmering mess of wholly conflicted emotions. She tried to crawl, to escape as best she could, but her bloody knee and twisted ankle brought an agonizing scream to her lips before she made it half a foot forward.

The murderer approached. Slower now, knowing his prey was all but caught. He'd killed Old Man Washington. Now he was after them. They must've gotten close. During her interviews with the townsfolk, with Huntley's help, they must've gotten close to discovering the identity of the elusive murderer. Who was he? What did he want? Why was he hellbent on killing an old man living alone in the middle of the woods and who was his next victim?

All these questions would go unanswered as soon as he--

He raised the knife, ready to slash down, to cut through her belly like nothing. From behind her, never leaving, never wavering, Huntley charged. He tackled the man despite the knife and they fell to the ground, the knife clattering away, not quite lost but no longer in anyone's possession.

"Go!" Huntley shouted. "Try, City Girl! My cabin's not far. Just... *go!*"

She cried from the pain, tears streaming down her cheek as the man she'd made love to tried to save her. Reaching for the pile of leaves in front of her, for anything, just to pull herself along a little bit further, her fingers wrapped around a perfect-sized piece of wood, a fallen branch from the tree at her side.

This would do. It would help. A walking stick to get her to Huntley's cabin. *Or...*

She used it to stand while the two men fought, grappling with each other, rolling through dew-wet leaves and scattered debris. Huntley had muscle and size at his command, but he wasn't an MMA fighter, he was a lumberjack. The other man had the element of surprise and a willingness to fight dirty. He tossed a spray of dirt and mud and crushed up leaves into the lumberjack's eyes, blinding him for a few precious seconds.

The shadowy man quickly grabbed the chef's knife, fingers wrapped tight around the handle. He moved to sink it into Huntley's back, over and over and over again, turning him into a bloody pin cushion.

Chantel lifted the perfect wooden walking stick high overhead and cracked it soundly against their attacker's skull. The man didn't budge at first, his body staying perfectly still, as if her attack hadn't been nearly enough to stop him. She dropped the stick, the sting of the hit throbbing through her tight fingers.

Their assailant fell to the ground with a thud, knocked out, the knife in his hands falling free.

Huntley rolled onto his back, gasping for air, staring up at her with adrenaline-infused eyes. It took them a second to realize what had happened, but once they did--

"Nice one, City Girl," Huntley said, lifting his hand in the air and giving her a thumbs up despite his exhaustion. "I always knew you were good for something!"

"Shut up!" she said, trying not to laugh, trying not to cry, failing at both simultaneously. "What do we do now?"

Suddenly someone else was in the woods with them. Chantel screamed as a second shadowy figure bullrushed her. She flung herself at Huntley who wrapped his arms around her, clinging to her for dear life, protecting her with his own burly body.

They stayed like that for a long few seconds. More. Longer.

Nothing happened.

When they finally eased up, when Huntley reluctantly let her loose from his bodyguard's embrace...

Both men were gone. The one who attacked them first and the one who'd rushed at them from out of nowhere. Just gone.

Nothing but the chef's knife was left behind to let her and her lumberjack know they hadn't dreamed this entire ordeal.

"Fuck," Huntley grunted, breathing hard. "Let's... get to my cabin first," he said, thinking as quickly as possible. "We should be safer there. Maybe not safe, but safer. I'll phone the sheriff. If we can hold out for an hour, he should be able to get here. Can you make it?"

"Yes," Chantel answered. "I think so. Let me just--"

She winced, trying to stay strong. It was a struggle but they managed to get to their feet. She grabbed the walking stick again, using it for leverage, and they slowly made their way to his cabin. It wasn't even fifty feet away, so very very close.

If only she hadn't tripped. If only she hadn't dropped her phone. If only she hadn't--

What was she even doing anymore? This wasn't what she'd signed up for. She'd come to the small town to work on a story, a freelance article for the newspaper she wrote for back in the city. Now she was fleeing through the woods in the middle of the night, making love to a lumberjack, nearly getting killed, trying to expose a murderer or two...

And for what? Why?

Huntley tucked her into bed, cocooning her in his blankets while he called the sheriff.

She didn't know what to tell him but she thought if they made it through the morning she'd try to explain why she really thought it was for the best if she went back home now...

The rest of the page in this document is blank.

CHARLOTTE

"Holy fucking shit," Hunter says once he finishes reading the newest addition to my story. "So, wait, there's *two* killers?"

I fidget next to him, unsure if I should tell him yet. Also, um... I haven't actually decided how I want to end it or if there's going to be another twist. I need to think it through more before I write that part.

"I... I can't tell you!" I say, rushed, mumbling the words under my breath as I try not to look at him in case he realizes I'm making everything up as I go at this point.

"Dude," Hunter says, staring.

I stick to what I'm doing, looking as far away from him as possible. I see him smirking out of the corner of my eye as I stare at the most interesting corner of the ceiling right over *there.* Yes, right there. It's, um... the corner where two walls meet and the ceiling's above them and, you know, that's how corners work, so...

We're back in my dorm room, sitting on my bed, sort of cuddled up together but not quite. I wrote a lot in the library and then I got hungry so Hunter and I went to the cafeteria for food first and he's been reading this entire time while I slowly nibbled on a fish sandwich. It's really good, one of those sandwiches on a brioche bun with fried fish and a little lettuce and tartar sauce. I've also barely eaten half of it because I keep getting nervous watching Hunter read my story.

The half I ate isn't even a full regular half, either. It's just the outer rim of the sandwich as I slowly spun it in a circle, nibbling the bun and little bits of the edge of the patty. Mostly the bun, though. The good part's always in the middle and I've neglected to eat any of that so far.

Hunter keeps staring at me until suddenly he doesn't and now he's looking at the plate in my lap.

"What'd you do to your fish sandwich?" he asks, looking at the half-eaten monstrosity I've somehow managed to create.

I blink and look down at it and it's just a little ball of what used to be a sandwich. It still kind of looks like a sandwich, but maybe it's a slider now? Less bun, a little too tall, forgotten pieces of shredded lettuce dangling down the sides, and, um... yes.

"I'm *nervous!*" I finally say, squeaking out the words.

I grab my sandwich and take a big bite and chew because that's how nervous I am. Do you understand now, Hunter?

"I don't know if you realize this, but yeah, it's *your* story so I don't know what you'd be nervous about?" he says, shrugging. "If you don't like something, just change it, you know?"

"I like it," I say, but my mouth is way too full and the words come out as "*Mf mfffff nghfm.*"

"Yeah?" Hunter says, laughing. "That so?"

I chew as fast as possible and then swallow, making sure I don't, um... I feel like it'd be just my luck if I choked on my dinner and ended up in the hospital, maybe in a coma or something, and never finished writing my story, so I try very very hard *not* to do that. I carefully swallow and glance at what's left of my sandwich while Hunter sits next to me, waiting for me to continue.

"I *like* it," I say, anxious. "I just don't know if *you* like it," I add. "Also, um... what if no one else likes it? What if it's really bad?"

"I like it so far," Hunter says. "I mean, it's a romance story so it's gonna have a happy ending, right? You're not killing off Huntley or anything?"

"Um, no, I wasn't planning on it," I say, still trying to keep my secret. "I... c-can I tell you something?"

"I thought that's what we've been doing this whole time so yeah?" Hunter says, snickering.

"Look, don't, um... d-don't tell anyone!" I stammer. "I... don't actually know who the murderer is yet..."

Hunter stares at me for a very long time and I'm pretty

sure this is the stare that's going to ruin me. Now he knows. He knows how bad I am at this. He has secret intimate knowledge about just how awful a writer I am because I don't even know how my own story ends. I should know who the murderer is, right? I mean, yes. I'm the person writing this story. I get to decide and I should've probably decided a long time ago, but it's hard, you know?

"Dude," Hunter says, wide-eyed and excited. "Fuck. Baby Sis! You're a goddamn genius!"

"I'm so sorry I know how bad this is!" I say, instinctive, ready to apologize for everything ever at the drop of a hat.

It takes me a second to realize he didn't tell me I'm bad at writing, though.

"Wait, um, I am?" I ask. "Why?"

"It's a mystery, right?" Hunter points out. "If even you don't know who killed Old Man Washington then nobody else is ever going to guess. I really like that, actually. I would've picked a murderer straight away but I'm pretty sure I would've fucked it up and made it obvious who it was before the end. Sort of kills the surprise, you know? Pun intended."

"I, um... what I was *going* to do," I say, excitedly nodding along. "I was going to--"

I tell him my evil plan.

I don't know who the murderer is yet, but I have a list of everyone in town that's appeared in the book so far. It'll definitely be one of them. It won't be a complete surprise or anything. And they each have a motive, right? Since this is my first draft, what I wanted to do was once I decide who the murderer is, when I'm editing it later, I'll go back and sneak in little hints but nothing too big.

So, um... Hunter's not reading that version but it'll basically be the same except with slight hints explaining everyone's possible motives so when someone else is reading it for the first time they'll have a lot of options as to who the murderer *could* be and once the big reveal happens they can point to the hints I laid out earlier in the book and, um... yes.

"I love it," he says, sincere, smiling. "That's really cool. Seriously. I'm not just saying that because we're alone in your dorm room."

"Wait, um, what's that have to do with anything?" I ask, confused.

"It was kind of a joke, but kind of not a joke?" he says, conflicted. "Like, you know... I'm not just agreeing with you because I'm trying to get in your pants, you know?"

"*Are* you trying to, um... to do that?" I ask, curious.

"Is that an option? You haven't even finished your food yet."

"Oh," I say. "Ummm..."

I chomp down on my fish sandwich and eat half of what's left. I don't chew like a madwoman this time and I take care to swallow properly, but there's not much left at this point and it's mostly the juicy moist fish in the middle, so...

A minute later I'm done. Hunter stares at my plate, impressed

"Now you have fish breath though," he points out.

"Hunter!" I whine. "You can't *say* things like, um... you're trying to get in my pants, and then *not* get in them. It's not nice. It's kind of mean, actually. I don't know if it's *rude*, but--"

Hunter smirks while I rant and I'm not really paying attention at this point so when he takes my empty plate and puts it on my desk, I don't realize it at first. When he does the same with my laptop, setting it next to my plate, I kind of realize it but I don't really know what's going on still.

I both realize it and don't realize it when he drags me down the bed while I'm still ranting and unbuttons my pants. When he tugs my pants down my legs I mostly realize it but I'm still ranting! Let me finish my--

I'm done, or I kind of am, when suddenly Hunter slides a finger up and down my lower lips above my panties. I gasp, eyes wider than ever, staring down at him as he settles between my thighs. And then, um... he tugs my panties to the side and tests my arousal with the tip of his finger. Finding me more than ready, wet and wanting, he, um...

He slips one finger inside me while I'm kind of still trying to remember what I was ranting about. Suddenly my hips buck up and my eyes roll into the back of my head and there's something about fishy breath but I don't even know what? Hunter doesn't bother taking my panties off, either. Nope. He pulls them as far to the side as he can, one finger pressed inside me, curling up and going straight for that perfect spot right *there*. His tongue crashes against my exposed clit and I frantically wriggle and writhe on the bed in a sudden spasmic dance of passion.

Oh gosh, what the heck is happening--

Hunter destroys me from the inside out, making quick work of my body, as if he knows every single thing about me, what I like, what'll send me over the edge the fastest, what he needs to do, exactly when and where, to bring me to a great big *O*.

Um, he does that. He also knows all those things. It's very impressive and if I were a college course he'd definitely pass. He's done the work, studied everything for this semester, and he may even be winning a prestigious award by the end of this.

I squirm on the bed, hips riding up and down, his tongue and his mouth pinning me to the bed while his finger works the other side. I gasp and shout out my ecstasy and suddenly it's happening, I'm cumming, and he's not stopping, not letting me stop. It goes on and on and...

I crash to my bed, exhausted, as Hunter laps up my wetness, his tongue enjoying my taste. He slides his tongue along either side of my lower lips, then the middle, all of me, tasting every inch of my pussy. Once he's done and satisfied, he drags his finger out and licks that, too.

I just kind of stare at him in an orgasm-induced daze, my pants gone, panties still on, and, um...

"Hi," I say, watching as he smiles at me, loving and sweet.

"Did it," Hunter says, winking. "Got in your pants. Happy now?"

"Um, yes, b-but..." I mumble, unsure if I should say this right now but feeling it so hard that my chest hurts. If I don't, I don't know what I'm going to do. If I don't say it, I...

Hunter grins, enjoying the moment. He slides up the bed, cuddling next to me, him in all his clothes, me in, um... you know, a shirt. I have socks on, too. I don't know if those count.

"I really do love your story," he says. "It's cool. I can't wait to read the rest."

"Right, um, so..." I mumble, wondering if I can play this off as a joke if I say it in a silly way. "Speaking of um, *that*, well... I... really do love, um... it's you. I love you?"

Hunter stares at me and I stare back and he's not laughing and I'm about to die of serious embarrassment if he doesn't say something soon. Please laugh! Or say it back? Or, um...

"Is it because I'm good with my tongue?" he asks, smirking.

"No, but that helps?" I offer. "It's, um... it's not the *reason* but I enjoy that, so..."

"Hey, guess what?"

"What?" I ask, still very confused.

"I love you, too," he says, leaning close, kissing me.

Oh gosh, that's a lot.

My chest still hurts but in a good way now, like I'm ready to fly and it's a little nerve-wracking but I know I can do it. My heart's not just going to run away on its own, I'm going with it, and we're going to fly and soar through the air together and we might fall a little bit sometimes, feeling that stomach dropping sensation, but it won't be forever or for long and I'm not going to crash land and, um...

I kiss him back and I frantically need to feel every inch of him, inside and out. I scramble with the buttons on his jeans and then the zipper and I pull them down just enough so I can sit in his lap and sink down his, um... his manhood... his shaft... his...

I do that, quick, practiced. I, um... I haven't practiced a lot but he just gave me an orgasm and I'm very wet and he hasn't had an orgasm yet so he's very hard. Basically it's all quite easy at this point and we kiss and I cling to him and I just stay like that, sitting in his lap, feeling him inside me. I squeeze and he throbs and that's about it. It's a lot, though.

"I do," I say, kissing his face everywhere. "I love you a lot, Hunter."

"I know," he says, grinning. "I love you so much, Charlotte."

"Can you, um... can you say the other name, too?" I ask. "Just so I know you love me all different ways?"

He laughs. "I guess?"

I can feel his laugh in his stomach as I sit on top of him and then I can feel it inside me as it crashes through the rest of his body. I can feel his laugh as it rolls up his shaft, directly inside me, as deep as it can go.

"I love you so much, Baby Sis," he says. "Charlotte. Charlie. Uh, what else?"

"That's good," I say. "That's enough."

I don't know where it comes from because we aren't even moving, but the feeling, the love, the sensation of kissing him and loving him and having him inside me, it's, um... it's very intense and it's a lot and now I'm--

I kiss him slowly, desperately slow, feeling every inch of his lips against mine as a quiet but oh so strong second O crashes through me. I feel myself clenching against him, against his shaft, as my body gives in to things I didn't even realize I was holding in before. I massage and squeeze and grip against him, just, um... sitting like that, on him, in his lap as he lays down, and then suddenly I feel him doing the same, returning those same feelings.

I feel him cumming, feel him pulsing and throbbing and trembling underneath and inside me as we share a wonderful beautiful moment. I think that's what this is. I *hope* that's what this is. I want it to be that so very very badly.

I collapse on top of him after and I know we probably need to get up and clean our mess and, um... Chloe could show up at any moment so we probably shouldn't be laying half naked on my bed because that's probably awkward.

Right, um, so...

"Yo," Hunter says, grinning as he brushes my slightly damp hair to the side, kissing my cheek. "Want to take a shower together? Gotta clean up, right?"

"Is this a sexy shower or a regular shower?" I ask, suspicious as to his intentions.

"I was thinking a romantic shower where we enjoy the romance and, you know, if I happen to slip inside you, well..."

"So very romantic," I say, giggling and rolling my eyes.

Hunter winks. "Yeah, the fish breath is definitely doing it for me, too."

"H-Hunter!" I gasp, trying not to laugh. I playfully smack his chest and, um... I get up off him except I forgot what's inside me and that kind of goes all over his stomach.

It's his own fault, though. He deserves it.

He mostly ignores it and chases me as I run around my room, laughing and trying to get away from him. It doesn't work for long and he catches me in about ten seconds but it's fun while it lasts. Hunter pulls me close and kisses me hard and, um... the mess I left on him is now on me too because he's grabbing my butt and it's impossible to get away from him.

I kind of like it, though. Not the mess part. The butt part. We can clean the mess up easily enough. It's fine.

"Hey, you ready for summer vacation soon?" he asks. "Also, fuck, Vegas! That's, uh... when again?"

"Next weekend," I say, smiling and kissing him quick. "Um, I think I am, but I don't know what to do in Vegas?"

"Just fun stuff, I guess," he says with a shrug. "There's a hotel with flamingos. Sounds cool."

"Real flamingos?" I ask, feeling like I'm getting my hopes up.

"Yeah, why would they have fake flamingos?"

"Flamingos!" I say, excited. "I want to see a flamingo."

"Calm your sexy ass down, Baby Sis," Hunter says, smacking said sexy ass immediately after. "Or don't. I love when you get excited. Hey, I love you too, by the way. In case I didn't get that point across yet."

"I love flamingos," I tell him. "Um, I also love you but I really want to see flamingos now."

"It's cool," Hunter says, chuckling. "Let's do it. Next weekend. Vegas. It'll be great."

"Okay," I say, nodding a whole lot of times.

And it *is* great, but also...

We aren't at this point yet but something happens while we're there and it's... it's bad...

I have no idea how we're supposed to explain this to our parents.

HOT GIRL SUMMER!

Episode 183

CHARLOTTE

ANGELA

"BABES! Hot girl summer is HERE! Are we ready for it?"

CLARISSA

"Oh my gosh I'm so excited oh my gosh oh my gosh oh my gosh!"

JENNY

"I'm totally ready, babes. I have my hot girl summer anthem picked out and everything. This is going to be great."

This is a text exchange in our girl power group chat and, um... that's Angela, Clarissa, and Jenny in that order.

I think I'm supposed to answer too so I reply with:

> "I haven't had a hot girl summer before. How hot is it going to be, though? I promise I'm excited but if it's too hot can we go somewhere with air conditioning?"

Angela answers first with:

ANGELA

"Charlie, babe, yes, for sure. Also, babes, we totally need to remember to put on sunscreen every few hours and stay hydrated, alright? Sunburns and skin cancer are bad, and I know sometimes it's tempting to, like, not drink as much water because you're having fun and sometimes you look extra toned and hot when you haven't had a lot of water in awhile, but it's totally not worth it, alright?

We're still hot even if we aren't extra toned looking! Hot girl summer is a mindset, not a physical look. Be hot in your mind and the rest will follow."

Clarissa has opinions on this:

CLARISSA

"I totally agree with everything you just said but is it okay if I'm also hot with my body and not just my mind? I want to go hard with sundresses and crop tops and the super short shorts where you can see the bottom of my bum because I've totally been doing squats and I just want people to know and appreciate that."

Jenny also has ideas about all of this:

JENNY

"I mean, babes? Babes. Totally for sure, babes. But seriously, I don't want to be that girl or anything, but come on, we're all definitely hot, physically and mentally and whatever other way there is, right?

I don't think we have anything to worry about. I appreciate your butt too, Clarissa. I see you, babe. That booty, am I right?"

CLARISSA

"Awww, thanks, Jenny! That means so much coming from you."

I, um... I'm a little lost at the moment and I don't know if I should also tell Clarissa her butt is looking good lately? I haven't actually noticed. I mean, she always looks super pretty and so does Angela and Jenny does too and, um... I mean, everyone does?

I don't understand what this has to do with summer and the weather, though.

Ohhhhh wait! I... I get it now...

It's not summer that's going to be hot. It's *us* that are going to be, um...

I have a lot of questions now:

"I understand what hot girl summer is now. Sorry, I got confused. And I'm really happy that everyone's excited but what happens if we aren't hot, though?"

Angela texts back with record speed:

ANGELA

"Wait, Charlie, who isn't hot? What's going on, babe?"

Clarissa adds:

CLARISSA

"I don't know either."

Jenny clarifies with:

JENNY

"I think Charlotte's trying to say she doesn't think she's hot but come on, babes, we all know she totally is, right? I mean, I don't know how she could even ask something like that after her pole dance where she completely dominated the entire competition, but I kind of get it. We all have doubts sometimes, right?"

I appreciate it but also:

"Thanks, Jenny. That's really nice but I don't know if it's true. You're all way prettier than me and I'm trying my best with makeup and everything but I don't know if I can wear crop tops and super short shorts that show off my bum yet, you know?"

Clarissa lets me know I can borrow a pair of hers anytime. Angela points out that it's not about the size of the bum but what you do with it. I don't even know what that means. I, um... I sit with my bum? What else am I supposed to do with it?

...Unless she's talking about things I could do with my butt when Hunter and I are, um... *you know...* in which case I can think of a few extra things but usually we aren't wearing clothes and I don't know how this is related to super short shorts.

Right, so, anyways--

ANGELA

"Look, babes, let's meet up this weekend, do some shopping on the cheap, grab a couple super hot summer outfits to cheer Charlie up, and, like, totally prepare for our epic roadtrip! We need to coordinate with the boys but I was thinking maybe plan for it in a couple weeks? Is that good for everyone?"

Clarissa's in:

CLARISSA

"Yes! Totally!"

Jenny's also onboard:

JENNY

"I'm in."

Me, though? Ummm... I haven't mentioned something to the girls yet...

"I can't this weekend. I'm going somewhere. Sorry."

I didn't think this was a big deal but suddenly I'm bombarded with texts asking where I'm going, why, what, who I'm going with, how I'm getting there, and, um... it's a lot. Oh gosh.

I answer as best I can, hoping I don't say too much on accident.

"My mom and Hunter's dad won a weekend trip to Las Vegas but they can't go so me and Hunter are going instead. It's just for the weekend. I can go shopping next week or any other time, though. Is that okay?"

Clarissa replies with:

CLARISSA

"Oh my gosh, Charlie, are you getting married?!"

Wait, what?

Angela adds:

ANGELA

"Totally fine, babe! Have fun with your man. We'll see you next week. Wait, are you getting married, Charlie?!"

Jenny's as confused as I am:

JENNY

"Why do you guys think she's getting married? Because she's going to Vegas?"

Just in case it needs to be said I text them back with:

"I'm not getting married. We need to pretend to be married to check in, though? The reservation is under our parents names so that's why."

ANGELA

"Oh. Good. Because if you don't invite us to your wedding, that's, like, totally unacceptable! LOL. JK, Charlie. I mean, I totally want to go and if you need bridesmaids or whatever, yes, PLEASE. But you do you, alright?"

That's Angela.

CLARISSA

"I want to be a bridesmaid!"

That's Clarissa.

JENNY

"Guys, she's not even getting married. She's just going to Vegas for the weekend. Shh."

That's Jenny.

"We did say I love you to each other the other night, though. But we haven't talked about getting married. I would let you know if we did. You can all come, I promise. How many bridesmaids are there usually? Can you all be bridesmaids?"

That's, um... that's me?

ANGELA

"Oh my gosh babes they said it!"

CLARISSA

"Yes, Charlie! Yes!"

JENNY

"You can have as many bridesmaids as you want, Charlotte. It's totally up to you."

Angela, Clarissa, and Jenny.
And then--

CHLOE

"Damn, sorry, I was working at the movie theatre and couldn't check my phone until now. Sorry, I would totally come but I can't do hot girl summer with you girls. Happy to go shopping, though! Oh, and have fun in Vegas, roomie! Don't accidentally get hitched! LOL. How funny would that be? So happy you and your hunky stepbrother are madly in love, by the way. Super cute!"

That's Chloe. She's also in the girl power group chat now. And, um...

HANNAH

"I'm not sure if I'm invited but if you guys have room can I be part of hot girl summer, too? I can do whatever. I was just going to spend the summer at home, so..."

That's Hannah, who is in the girl power group chat now, too.

Clarissa texts back with:

CLARISSA

"Roxy! Yes! Love you, Hannah!"

Angela confirms:

ANGELA

"Hannah, babe, YES. You're one of us. Never doubt that. Love your nose ring, babe. I wasn't too into it at first because it's a little different but I've totally been thinking maybe I should get one now? Like, not the kind you have, but a cute little stone for my nostril, you know? What do you think? Let's talk more about hot girl summer and accessories during our shopping trip, babe."

And so it's decided. We're going shopping, but not until I get back from Las Vegas with Hunter. Which, um... speaking of...

"Babies!" my mom says, pulling me and Hunter into a hug as soon as we step foot in the door. "Oh my gosh I missed you so much. Look how grown you two are now! How are you? I haven't seen you in forever. Have you been eating? Do you need food? Your new stepdad is getting some as we speak! That's your father, Hunter. I don't have a new new man. It's the same new one as always, but I just love saying that, you know?"

"Figured," Hunter says, being hugged.

He's doing his best not to give in to my mom's attempt at turning us into one big happy family. I think because, um... you know, him and I are dating and we've had sex a bunch of times and that might be awkward.

I hug my mom back because she's my mom, though. I don't know what to do with Hunter so I nervously pat him on the head. He looks at me, brow furrowed, nose scrunched up, both slightly annoyed but mostly he's trying not to laugh.

"Okay, so, Vegas!" my mom says, leading us to the couch. "Let's talk about this. Are you ready? It's only for the weekend so you don't have to pack a lot. Overnight bags are fine. But, oh! One thing, baby," she says specifically to me. "Sometimes those security men are prickly about makeup, so if you're bringing any then maybe you two should plan on checking a bag at the airport, alright?"

Hunter turns to me with a wicked grin on his face. "*Are* you planning on bringing any makeup, Baby Sis?"

...I have no idea what that means but, um...

"Yes?" I answer, feeling all the while like I'm saying something wicked and naughty somehow.

I don't even know why! What's wrong with makeup, Hunter? It's not *just* for you. In fact, the cheerleaders and Jenny totally agree that makeup is for ourselves and if boys happen to like it, well, so be it. And, um, hot girl summer? I think. I don't know if that's a reason yet or not.

"It's so nice to get all dolled up for a night out," my mom says, wistful. "When I first met your new stepdad, I was dressed to kill with hot red lipstick to prove it! Let's just say, your father appreciated that later on. Now it's one of our things. I had to reapply it a couple times that night and we never even left the room. I won't say more. I know you two don't want to hear that. But, woo boy..."

"...Mom," I mumble, flat. I don't know exactly what she means but I'm pretty sure it's a sex thing.

"Yeah, uh..." Hunter adds, in full agreement.

"Just teasing, you two! You're so funny. You take everything so seriously. I love how well you get along, though. This is going to be so fun for the both of you! I'll let you pack. You need to pack, right? You have about twenty minutes until your father gets back with the food, babies. You can use my luggage set upstairs if you need to, alright? Go! Be free! Vegas!"

My mom lifts her hands in the air while she slowly nudges us to the stairs. Once we take the hint and start to walk up, she keeps her arms spread wide and wanders from the front of the house to the kitchen, exactly like that. I didn't realize sending us on a weekend getaway to Las Vegas was so, you know... exciting? My mom is super excited about this, more excited than I've ever seen her about anything in my life.

As soon as she's out of view, Hunter grabs my hand and tugs me upstairs. I have my book bag slung across my back and he has his and, um...

We make a beeline for my bedroom. As soon as we're inside, he quickly shuts the door behind us, shrugs his bag off, grabs mine, tosses both onto my bed, and pins me up against the wall.

"I mean this in the nicest and most romantic way possible, but I can't fucking wait to have you all to myself for the weekend," Hunter says, staring down at me, his lips so close to mine I can practically kiss them.

I try to do that but he smirks and pulls away slightly.

"Okay!" I say, nodding, still not able to kiss him yet.

"Shit, that's it?" he asks with a smirk.

"Okay you can have me all to yourself this weekend?" I

say, in case that part wasn't as obvious as I thought. "Wait! Do, um... do I get you all to myself, too?"

"Yeah," he says.

"Okay!"

"I don't know why but I thought there'd be a little more to it?" Hunter says, conflicted. "Like, uh..."

"We have toys?" I offer.

"We do..." he says, trailing off.

We glance towards my illicit book bag, the one that looks so sweet and innocent, but is currently stuffed full with a handful of toys we picked specifically for our weekend getaway. We snuck into the art club storage room before heading back to my mom's place, tossed some of the items from the *"Yes, Please"* section of my secret toy box into my bag, and, um... that's it.

We need to have everything out of our dorms by the end of next week so we're going to wait a little while and figure out how best to move my toy box back home so my mom doesn't see it. We both figured it'd be easier to sneak it somewhere if we brought it with the rest of our stuff? We don't have a ton of stuff, but we have enough that it's slightly less obvious what's inside any one particular box if, um... if we put it alongside a bunch of other boxes?

...I have no idea what I'm supposed to do with the framed poster hanging in my dorm room of Hunter and I doing potentially dirty things, but we're going to figure that out at the same time...

"Okay, so..." Hunter says, unpinning me from the wall.

I snatch his hand quick as he leaves and he smiles back at me. We step over to my bed and my discreet book bag to take stock of our weekend getaway toy inventory.

I don't even know if we can use all of these this weekend but I guess we can try? Or we can make it a surprise. Or, um... I... I don't really know but I'm super excited and I really want to know what *that* one's like--

It's the first thing Hunter pulls out of my bag, a small, innocuous package containing a ring about two inches around with this sort of rectangular-ish shaped part at the top. It's one seamless piece of silicone, the ring part wide enough to fit a certain masculine piece of equipment that I'm becoming very fond of, and, um... the top part has a charging hole plug and then a button on the side and that's it.

It's a cock ring and I literally have no idea how it works but apparently it fits around Hunter and then it turns on and buzzes so I can pretend his penis is a vibrator?

I just think that sounds like a lot of fun and I want to try it please...

"Dude, you're drooling," Hunter says, smirking as I stare at the still-packaged toy in his hand.

"I... I am not!" I mumble, swiping at my mouth with the back of my hand to check.

And, um... I'm not. Oh good. I was worried for a second.

Hunter laughs and tosses the cock ring package on the bed, out in the open for anyone to see. My cheeks immediately burn red and I glance towards the door just in case.

"Twenty minutes, remember?" he points out. "We're fine."

"...Okay," I say, nodding.

I pull out the next thing which is the set of um... it's ben wa balls? They go inside me. I don't know how those work either but Hunter thought they'd be fun to try out?

I pretend to casually toss them on the bed like I don't even care and I do this all the time but I'm nervous and I throw them way too hard. They clank against the wall and then slide between the wall and the side of my bed, falling underneath.

"Nooooo!" I squeak, flinging myself on the bed to--

I don't actually know. I just kind of fling myself on the bed, stomach down, rear up. I realize the error of my ways as soon as Hunter's palm smacks my butt.

"H-Hunter!" I shriek, flopping on my bed, spinning around fast.

Now I'm on my back but this isn't much better. Hunter's at the side of the bed, staring down at me. He presses between my slowly opening thighs. They honestly have a mind of their own right now and my legs just seem to spread as soon as Hunter comes anywhere near me in certain positions. What's going on and why is this happening with me? I don't actually mind but if someone could explain it to me that'd be great.

He presses one knee between my legs, then the other, coming close, crawling further and further up alongside my body. He's so close now and he's above me and if we weren't wearing all our clothes I'd think we were about to, um... s-s-sex stuff, and...

Slow, deliberate, he reaches between my bed and the wall. The ben wa balls apparently didn't fall all the way to the floor and got stuck halfway down on my bedframe. Hunter drags them up, his eyes locked with mine the whole time, then he neatly places my toy in my loose, fumbling hand before pushing himself up and off the bed, back to his feet.

"Don't want to lose those, now do we?" he says, the most stupidly seductive growl in his voice.

How does he *do* that? I wish I could do that. Maybe a purr instead of a growl.

I try it in case I *can* do it and I don't realize it, and, um...

"Noooooooo," I say, hoping this is purry but I don't know how. "We do *nottttttt...*"

That's not it, is it?

Hunter grins and lets me try my best, though. I like that.

He takes my hand, pulling me to my feet again. We take my favorite rabbit vibe out of my book bag because that's in there, too. And then, um... there's the pair of vibrating panties. I don't know if we're actually ever going to use those but if there's ever a time it's when we're in Vegas maybe? I don't know why. That's just what people say, right? I don't know *who* says it, but, um...

Shhhhhhhhhh!

Hunter goes to my mom's room for the aforementioned luggage set. We don't need a lot so he just brings back this little hardback suitcase that can hold a few things in case we want a checked bag. Which, um... I think we do because please don't make me go through the security queue with a vibrator and other assorted sex toys.

I haven't flown a lot and every time I have it's always been fine if not absolutely nerve-wracking. I don't even know why I get so nervous. My worst nightmare is not only getting stopped at the X-ray machine, but for some reason they find something in my carry-on bag and, um... it's bad. It's very bad.

I don't even know *what* it is, or I didn't before, but now I do.

They'll find my toys, but they won't *know* they're toys at first, you know? So this is basically what my worst fear is now, as presented by my wild imagination:

I get to the front of the line and I go through and I don't know why but Hunter and I decided to try out the ben wa balls on the flight. So, you know, I'm... wearing them... inside me... and, um...

"What's that?" the person manning the machine says, pointing something out to his co-worker.

"Shit, this is bad," the man he works with says.

"Miss, if you could come out here and step to the side, please?" the first man says. "No need to be alarmed..."

Except suddenly everyone in a TSA uniform looks like they're on high alert.

"Her bag, too," the woman checking carry-on luggage says.

"Shit," the second man says again.

"This is *bad*," the first says, again, in case everyone else didn't realize it yet.

"Shut everything down!" a supervisor calls out. "We have a Code Eight emergency!"

"H-Hunter!" I cry out as I'm pulled away to explain myself except it's just sex toy stuff and oh my gosh I'm in so much trouble, aren't I?

So then they interrogate me in a private room about the, um... you know, balls that showed up on the scan.

"*This*, too," a woman says, fishing through my bag and pulling something out, slamming it down on the table next to me.

It's a remote. It's the remote to the pair of vibrating panties Hunter and I decided to bring, packed in my carry-on instead of our shared checked bag.

"It's, um... it's not what it looks like!" I say, trying to explain.

"Miss Scott, I don't know if you realize this, but you're in some potentially *serious trouble*," the supervisor says, taking charge. "Now, if you come clean, we may be able to help you. You were traveling with a man, were you not? Does he have anything to do with this?"

I mean, yes, technically he does, and I'm beyond nervous right now, so, um...

"...Yes?" I say.

"Cuff him!" the supervisor says. "Bring him here!"

So then they drag Hunter in and I don't know if he thinks I'm a terrible criminal or if he's realized what's going on but...

"It's... it's... it's s-s-sex toys!" I somehow manage to stammer out.

Then everyone stares at me, giving me empty, blank faced looks. The woman with my bag continues to fish through it, not only finding the vibrating panties but my favorite rabbit vibe, too. And, um...

"...We thought it'd be fun to spice things up," Hunter

informs them. "With, uh, you know... she's wearing some kegel balls? Inside her? Yeah..."

So that's how that goes in my head, this entire made up nightmare scenario of what I definitely don't want to happen when going through airport security. Oh, and they also inform the entire airport that it was a false alarm and it was just some girl's sex toys, which everyone laughs about and somehow they all know it's me and then there's an article posted in the newspaper the next day with my burning red blushing face on the front page.

GIRL AND HER STEPBROTHER GET PULLED ASIDE IN AIRPORT SECURITY LINE FOR SEX TOY SCANDAL IN CARRY-ON BAGS

That's what the headline will be. I know it's kind of long, but, um...

"Dude," Hunter says, nudging my shoulder as I daydream about all of this while sitting on my bed back home. "Did you hear me?"

"Um, no," I say, shaking myself out of it.

"I put the toys in the checked bag and we can toss some other stuff like your makeup and toothpaste or whatever in too, but we should probably add a few clothes or something so everything's not bouncing all around in there, you know?"

"Oh good," I say. No longer do I fear being pulled aside in airport security. "W-wait!" I add, panicking. "Um, did you..."

I don't know how to explain this properly so I snatch my rabbit vibe out of the suitcase and push some buttons until a light on it blinks a couple times.

"Uh...?" Hunter asks, staring at me.

"It's, um... travel mode?" I say. "So it doesn't accidentally turn on when we're traveling..."

"Shit, good looking out," Hunter says, kissing me on the cheek.

"Also please I don't want to put the kegel balls in before going through airport security!" I add, just in case, you know, just in case...

"As *hilarious* as that sounds..." Hunter says, smirking. "Nah, it's cool. I would never do that to you."

"Seriously, this causes me anxiety," I tell him. "It's, um... it's bad."

"Is that why you were staring at nothing for five minutes just now?"

I nod. "Um, yes. Don't tell anyone, though."

"Your secret's safe with me," he says.

We pack some clothes quick, tossing a few thicker items in with the checked bag stuff to keep it protected, then filling up a duffle bag with a few pairs of clothes each. Oh, and bathing suits. I, um... I have a lot of bathing suits now and we have a hot tub in our room and...

Do I *need* to wear a bathing suit in the hot tub in our room?

No, I don't think so.

Do I *want* to because I want to tease Hunter and make him, um... I mean, he won't have to work that hard but maybe he can work a little bit and that'll be fun?

Yup, I do.

Oh, and flamingos.

"You weren't lying about the flamingos, right?" I ask him.

"Dude, why would I lie about flamingos?"

I shrug. "I don't know."

Also suddenly my mom's standing in the door. I didn't even realize she was there or that she'd opened it. I nervously glance at the hardback suitcase but thankfully it's zipped up shut and there's no way she can see what's inside.

"The flamingos!" my mom says, excited. "Yes! Babies. Please. Take pictures. Your dad wasn't that interested in seeing them, Hunter. I don't know why. He said they're just flamingos? As if there's nothing exciting about flamingos."

"There is!" I say, excited. "Flamingos are very exciting."

"I know, right?!"

...I don't know what exactly is exciting about them, but, listen... they just are.

"Good choice, by the way," my mom says, nodding to the suitcase. "Usually I use that one for my... well, let's just say I like to make sure I'm entertained on vacation! Ha! Your father calls it my toy box, Hunter. Isn't that funny? He's so funny sometimes."

I sit there, cheeks flush, trying not to give myself away, staring at the wall, hoping beyond hope my mom doesn't ask us to open it for whatever reason.

"Yeah, uh, we just have clothes..." Hunter mutters under his breath.

"And toothpaste," I add.

"And makeup," Hunter says.

"And Scrabble," I continue, because I don't know how to stop and I'm apparently very bad at this.

Hunter stares at me like I'm insane and I fully accept and understand this.

"Ha!" my mom laughs. "So you're bringing toys too? Aww, so cute! That's not quite what I meant, but I love it. Sometimes it's nice to end the day with a little game fun here and there, isn't it? Remember when we used to play boardgames before going to bed, honey?"

"That was a long time ago," I say. "But it was really nice."

"Good," my mom says, smiling. "Take care of my baby for me, Hunter. Alright? I'm going to miss you two! Make sure you play some games before bed. You two get along so well. I love it. I just absolutely love it. It's so nice and sweet. Oh, and the food's here! That's what I came up to tell you. Sorry for barging in like that. What if I'd caught you two doing something embarrassing? Ha! I know that would never happen. You're both good kids."

"Um... yup..." I mumble, because I'm very unsure about so many things right now and I don't know what else to say.

We really do have to tell our parents at some point. About us dating. And, um... I don't know if my mom will think we're good kids after that. I don't really know *what* she'll think, but...

"We'll be right down," Hunter says, answering for the both of us. "Almost done."

"We got pizza from that place you love," my mom adds. "And those loaded waffle fries! How good are those?"

I nod, trying to look excited, but I'm suddenly really nervous about everything all over again. Um, not about the weekend Las Vegas trip. More about what we need to do *after* that.

My mom leaves, closing the door behind her.

As if reading my mind, Hunter says, "Look, I know we have to tell them soon, but let's not worry about it this weekend, alright?"

"Okay," I say, swallowing hard, trying to sort through the thoughts in my head. "Do you think they'll be mad, though?"

"Nah, I'm sure it'll be fine," Hunter says, way too confident.

He says it with confidence, at least. I'm not sure the look in his eyes says the same thing. He's nervous just like me.

I, um... I have an idea, though...

When we get back. Later. This weekend is just for the two of us.

Yay, flamingos!

And toys.

And hot tubs?

And, um... I don't know what else yet but we're about to find out.

VEGAS, BABY!

Episode 184

CHARLOTTE

MOM

"Baby! The hotel is amazing. You're going to love it. I've never stayed at the Metropolitan but it's one of the Harriott Signature Collection hotels. How amazing is that?! I know, right? Me and your new stepdad met at the Wdara right behind it if you and H want to check out where the magic started happening between your parents. LOL! Anyways, you're going to have a blast. I promise! Don't forget to text me to let me know how everything's going."

"Oh, and absolutely don't forget you need to pretend to be me when you check in, baby! I know how nervous you get sometimes, so maybe let H do the talking? It's just for checking in, though. You should be fine after that! Have a great time, eat good food, try a buffet, maybe go see Barry Manilow in concert if he's there. I used to have such a crush on him back in the day. Don't even get me started! Alright bye now! Love you, baby!"

These are the last two texts my mom sent me before Hunter and I got on the plane for our six hour flight to Las Vegas. I didn't realize it would take that long to get there, to be honest. I think the time zone difference helps? When we land, it's not too late, and, um... to be honest, I kind of accidentally fell asleep halfway through the flight and when I woke up I was maybe possibly, um...

"I can't believe you drooled on my shoulder," Hunter says, teasing me as the taxi from the airport pulls off the road to the entrance loop just outside the Metropolitan.

"...I didn't drool!" I protest.

I actually did drool but it wasn't that much and I really didn't mean to. I was *sleeping,* Hunter! Don't make fun of me...

"You're lucky I like you," he says, smirking at me as the taxi driver ignores us completely.

"Um, excuse me but that's a downgrade..." I point out. "Please fix."

"So demanding," Hunter says, a playful snort. "You're lucky I *love* you. There. Happy now?"

"Yes. Thank you!"

I'm not that nervous yet except the further down this very large hotel driveway we get, the more I start to wonder why a hotel even needs a driveway this long? I'm used to, um... you know... whenever my mom and I would go on roadtrips when I was younger, because we usually couldn't afford to fly anywhere, we'd find these cute, possibly haunted, slightly dated and rundown, but still cute, um... they were just roadside motels.

My mom liked to find ones where the rooms were inside the building, though. She didn't like the motels with doors that opened up onto outside walkways. I don't know if there's a major difference between inside hallway rooms or rooms that open onto an outside walkway, or what the difference between a hotel and motel actually is now that I think about it.

We'd just walk into the lobby, no reservations booked beforehand, ask at the front desk if they had a room, which they somehow always did, pay on the spot, head to our room, and after lugging our bags up we'd look for the nearest twenty-four hour diner and have a nice hot meal before going back to the room to watch TV and get a good night's rest.

The next morning we'd be on the road by sunrise and if the diner was really good the night before we'd go there for breakfast, too. Otherwise we'd stop at a gas station on the way and grab something to eat in the car.

That's the extent of my vacation stay experiences in life thus far. My mom and I never stayed at hotels when we got to where we were going. We'd stay with relatives or my mom's friends and, um... that's an entirely different story that I really don't want to talk about right now, but, anyways--

Finally after driving down the hotel driveway for what seems like way longer than necessary, the taxi driver pulls up to this monstrously large, tinted glass front entrance. It reminds me of the entrance to the mall back home, except about five times bigger.

I stare, suddenly realizing what I've gotten myself into and why I should be nervous. There's blue and black glass as far as the eye can see, the sides of the Metropolitan literally made out of it. Most of it's dark and tinted, impossible to see what's on the other side, but the glass near the lobby is opaque enough that I can catch a small glimpse of the sinfully bright debauchery going on inside.

Mostly it's people walking through the lobby to wherever else, but I'm pretty sure they're going to do something really sinful because this is Las Vegas, you know?

Wait, are Hunter and I supposed to be sinful and debauched now? I, um... maybe?

Okay, deep breaths, Charlotte. In, out, breathe--

Before I have a chance to calm down, this random man in a suit with a dark cap opens the taxi door to kidnap us or steal our things. I balk and crash against Hunter, trying to escape my sinful fate or, um...

"Welcome to the Metropolitan!" the man says, cheerful as anything. "Do you have a reservation with us?"

I stare up at him as he greets us and open my mouth to say something but nothing comes out.

"Yeah," Hunter says. "All set with that. Thanks."

"Great," the man says. "Let me help you with your bags, sir."

The taxi driver up front huffs at us, pointing to the flat rate sign on his dashboard. Hunter takes out his dad's credit card and swipes it after the man grunts and pulls out his card machine to run our fare. He sounds very angry even though we just paid him and gave him a tip and I don't understand why. Is it because of the drool? It wasn't a lot and I only did it on the airplane, I promise!

Anyways, right, um...

I shuffle out of the taxi after we're paid up and the man who opened the door earlier already has our bags from the trunk ready and waiting at his side. Hunter nods and quietly gives the man some money for, um... I'm not entirely sure but my mom and his dad made sure we had some cash on hand so we could do just that.

We're both barely out of the taxi when the driver peels off

to go do whatever he needs to do. Whatever it is, I think he's late for it.

"Right this way," our apparent personal concierge says, leading us to the front of the massive entryway.

Two huge glass doors slide apart just for us as we make our way into the hotel. I switch between wide-eyed gaping at how stupidly fancy everything is and, um... rushing over to Hunter, snatching his arm, and holding it tight so I don't get left behind. Hunter snickers at me as the man with our bags takes us to the front desk where a woman's waiting for us.

"I have a--" he starts to say, nodding to me and Hunter.

"Um, I'm Charlotte?" I say, already forgetting the one thing I needed to remember. "I mean, Barbara! Bunny. My... my friends call me Bunny... b-but I'm Barbara and, um... Charlotte's a really nice name, isn't it?"

"Dude..." Hunter grunts, rolling his eyes at me.

"S-sorry!" I mumble.

"Jackson," Hunter says to the woman running the check-in desk, smooth, like he's a British secret agent, definitely a man of mystery. "We have a reservation under Dave Jackson and Barbara Scott."

The man with our bags tips his hat to the woman, who nods back to him, some secret message situation going on between them. I don't know if this is a fancy hotel thing or just a Metropolitan thing or a Las Vegas thing, but I kind of wish I could nod at someone like that and they just knew what I was saying. It seems very useful, you know?

"Ah, here we go!" the woman says after typing away on her computer. "Oh, wow. I see you two were the prize winners of the Luxury Weekend Slots jackpot awhile back. Congratulations and thank you for joining us at the Metropolitan Signature hotel!"

"...Thanks..." I mumble, as if we deserve the praise.

To be fair, does anyone really deserve praise for winning a

slot machine jackpot prize? You kind of just pull a lever and hope for the best, right?

"Now, as per the rules and regulations, and hotel custom, I'll need to ascertain that you are who you say you are," she says, giggly and free. "Plus I'll need a credit card to put on file. This is purely for security deposit purposes. Don't worry, you shouldn't actually be charged anything and the pending charge will fall off your card statement a few days after your stay. We'll be comping most of your hotel expenses besides any casino spend you may make while you're with us! We do hope you'll enjoy our casino, though. It's one of the best in Las Vegas, with every kind of machine and table you could dream of. What's your game of choice?"

I didn't realize we were going to be quizzed. Is this a part of it? Will they know I'm not my mom if I answer incorrectly?

Hunter's busy, too. He's searching through his wallet for his ID. Um, his dad's ID. Our parents gave us their drivers licenses before we left so we could pretend to be them while checking in. The woman behind the counter waits, patient for the time being, but how long will she stay that way?

I need to do something, or at least I think I do, so I say the first thing that comes to mind.

"Um, we b-both like to play Super Smash Hero sometimes?" I answer. "I don't know if that's my f-favorite game, but, um... I usually beat Hunter so. Dave! I meant Dave! I usually beat *Dave.* We... we have pet names for each other. They sound like completely different names, but it's just our pet names... for each other... and, um..."

Hunter stares at me as if we're both about to get kicked out of the hotel, sent back to the airport, and we'll have to fly another six hours to get home because I just screwed everything up. I mean, I did just screw everything up but it's not my, um... okay, it *is* my fault but this is really hard for me, alright?

Being Chantel in a stripclub was so much easier. I had

time to prepare. I knew what I was doing. I had support from my friends. I had nine inch stripper heels.

Yes, they were difficult to walk in, but they were still nice and I appreciate Bella letting me use her special shoes.

"I love that game!" the woman says, all smiles. "We don't have it in the casino, unfortunately. I wish we did. We occasionally hold eSports events and if you're interested in that we have a gambling desk dedicated towards making wagers for online competitions, but as far as I know there's nothing going on with that right now. I can check for you if you'd like, though?"

"Uh, no, we're good," Hunter says, handing over his dad's ID and credit card.

I give the woman my mom's ID as well. I found it while Hunter was giving me a death stare. She takes both, types in a few things, checks her computer screen, and then hands the cards back.

"I get what you mean about using other names sometimes," she says, casually making idle chit chat while getting our room reservation sorted out. "My boyfriend and I like to roleplay to spice up our relationship every so often. Nothing too scandalous, but I'll head to the bar before him and act like I'm single and ready to mingle, you know? I just love that phrase, don't you? He'll show up ten minutes later and chat me up like we're meeting for the first time and we spend the evening like that. It's really fun. I don't even know why. You have to mix things up every now and then, you know?"

"Yeah, we love mixing it up," Hunter says. "Right, Bunny? What kind of roleplay are you into, honey buns?"

"Um... I... I'm..." I mumble.

H-Hunter! You're mean. Ugh. It takes me a second of awkwardly standing there before finally thinking of something.

"I write romance stories," I say, which is true. "And, um...

sometimes *Dave* helps me by pretending to be the hero of my story and I pretend to be the heroine so, um... it's just so I can figure out ideas for a scene I want to write, you know?"

"Oh my gosh that's so cool!" the woman says. I don't know if she's actually excited or just being nice. "Tell me about your stories. What are you writing about right now?"

I don't know if she regrets this by the end but that single question leads me on a winding spiral of rambling as I explain everything about Chantel, the city girl journalist who goes to a small town to write a special article for the paper she works for, and shortly after arriving she meets Huntley, the hunky lumberjack who just so happens to live in a cabin near the one she rented for the week. Oh and there's a mysterious murder, so she decides to investigate that, and Huntley helps, and a lot of crazy stuff happens, and they realize they kind of like each other a lot, but then the murderer is coming for them and--

"That's as far as I am right now," I say, still excited. "Um, I'm almost finished writing it, though."

"It's really good," Hunter says.

"Is it going to be published anywhere?" the check-in desk woman asks. "I want to read it now."

"Um, no," I say, possibly destroying her hopes and dreams.

"It's not *not* going to be published somewhere," Hunter adds, hyping me up. "She's, uh... what are you going to do when you're done, Bunny? Shop around for an agent or go the indie publishing route or what?"

"Um, no?" I say. I don't understand the question. I literally have no idea what I'm going to do with the story. I just want to finish writing it first.

"You could get some paperback copies printed?" the woman behind the desk offers. "It's pretty affordable nowadays if you just want to get a few books printed. I have a friend who did it and gave them to people as a cute little Christmas gift."

...That sounds so cool...

"Do you, um... do you know how she did it?" I ask.

"I can ask her and get back to you?" the woman says.

"Yes, please!"

"Sure! Once I have the info, I'll have a member of the concierge team leave a note under your door. And... speaking of... here are your access cards for the illustrious Pomegranate Suite! It's our once-in-a-lifetime luxury honeymoon suite and it's absolutely to die for. Seriously, you're going to love it. It says here in my notes that you two were recently married within the past six months and you met in Las Vegas? Wow! This must be a dream come true for you."

"Um, n--" I start to say, forgetting, almost completely ruining it again. Hunter stares at me and reminds me what we're doing, though. "--Yes."

It kind of comes out as "Um, nyes" and I know it's not perfect but I didn't screw up too bad, right?

"That's so cute and fun," she says. "Okay, here you go! As I said, most of your expenses will be comped in accordance with the rules and regulations of your jackpot prize winnings. You can check and confirm that with any of our hotel concierge staff. The desk is right over there and they'll have access to everything on your account if you just show them your keycard. The casino is still full price, *but* the hotel manager would like to meet with you later and offer you a modest amount of free play for you to try out some of our machines. Someone should be around shortly to explain that to you after you get to your room. We try to keep things easy here, so you can load money onto your keycard as well. Then all you have to do is swipe or tap in the casino and you're good to go. If you need to cash out your winnings, you have to go to one of the service desks in the casino, but otherwise everything gets added to your personalized account so you can keep playing."

She says most of this in a single breath, practiced and perfect.

"Got it," Hunter says with a nod. "Thanks a lot. We really appreciate it."

He hands her some money for her trouble which, um... I think it's me. I'm the trouble. She smiles and accepts the folded up bills politely, folding it even further and putting it in her pocket with maximum efficiency.

"Oh, and I really do want a copy of your book if you print any!" she says, waving excitedly to me. "Chantel and Huntley sound absolutely *dreamy.* I can't wait. I'll have that info up to you soon."

"Okay!" I say, excited, waving back. "Um, thank you for everything."

"Of course! You're welcome," she says. "Bye now!"

"Bye!"

Hunter doesn't say bye. He just takes my hand and leads me away.

"Um, you didn't say bye?" I point out as we head to the elevators. "She was nice?"

"I don't want to ruin this for you, but I think everyone in Las Vegas is nice?" he says with a shrug. "Like, uh... they want our money so they're nice and hope we give it to them?"

"We did, though," I add. "We gave it to her. Um, you did, I mean."

"I meant more like... look, I'm not sure she actually wants a copy of your book?"

"...But she said she did..." I mumble, suddenly kind of sad if that's true.

"She might want one?" he offers, trying to cheer me up. "Just don't get offended if she was just being nice? That's all."

"I'm not offended, but I'm kind of sad," I say, deciding to say that part out loud.

"On the plus side, if she comes through and tells you about that print thing, you could get copies made for the romance book club?"

...I have no idea if this is an *absolutely amazing* idea or a wholly terrifying one...

On the one hand, oh my gosh, that'd be so fun. On the other hand, then all the romance book club girls would want to read my book for one of our club meetings and, um...

"Alright," Joanna would say. "As usual, let's start with everyone's favorite steamy scene! Who wants to go first?"

Silence. I imagine silence as no one says anything because my steamy scenes are bad and no one has a favorite.

...*Yup.*

"Stop that," Hunter says, bopping me on the head as I daydream about the worst case scenario. "I don't know what you're worrying about but your book is pretty cool and the girls would love it. Be confident, yo!"

"I'm so c-confident!" I say, doing my best. "...Yo..."

"You didn't have to add the yo part," Hunter says, laughing.

"I wanted to sound more confident?"

"It was real fucking cute, so I'll allow it," he says, laughing more.

We get into the elevator, then the tenth floor hallway, and finally all the way to our room before I belatedly realize we don't have our bags. Oh no.

Except, um... as soon as Hunter opens the door to the Pomegranate Suite...

It has a picture of a pomegranate on the door and everything. So this must be it but I don't know how.

Our bags are right inside the door, but it takes me about twenty minutes to see them because what the heck I think they gave us the wrong room.

This isn't even a room, it's a mansion?

It's... it's huge...

WELCOME TO THE POMEGRANATE SUITE

Episode 185

HUNTER

A lright, look, this is my first time in Vegas, too. I don't know what the fuck I'm doing. All I know is we're supposed to pretend to be our parents so we can check into the hotel.

I think that part's done and everything's smooth fucking sailing from here on out but as soon as I open the door to our room, which, you know, it's supposed to be a room, right? We're in a hotel. They have hotel *rooms*. That's the entire point of staying in a hotel.

Except, nah, not even close.

I open the door to what's supposed to be our room and there's a long hallway leading to who the fuck knows where instead? Baby Sis and I stare down the hall, presumably both of us having the same idea at the same time. The only saving grace is the fact that our luggage is tucked away right inside the door, so...

Honestly, I don't know if that makes any of this better.

"Is this our room?" my stepsister asks, leaning in as if she can figure it out by looking down the hall just a little bit more. "It, um... it doesn't look like a room?"

"It's definitely a hallway," I tell her.

She nods and steps back and I shut the door so we can figure this out. I don't know how. I'm winging it and hoping for the best.

Anyways, I look at our keycard again, the one with a stylized pomegranate on it, and it clearly states this is the key to the Pomegranate Suite. On the door in front of me, the one we just closed, there's also a pomegranate. It's the same goddamn pomegranate. And, you know, in case that wasn't clear enough, it says **"POMEGRANATE SUITE"** right under the image of a pomegranate, so...

I try the keycard again, listening to the door unlock a second time. It still works. The keycard for the Pomegranate Suite definitely unlocks the door in front of us.

"Um, what are you doing?" Baby Sis asks. "We just did that?"

"You know that horror movie we watched where they were trapped in a house in the middle of nowhere but every time they opened a door it led to somewhere different?" I say.

"Yes," she answers. "It was called Doors. I didn't really understand how that one was supposed to be scary, though?"

"Yeah, not sure. I mean, they were just lost in a house and kept getting split up but that was it. Anyways, maybe this is like that?"

"...Is the hotel haunted?" Baby Sis asks, clearly skeptical. "I don't think fancy hotels are supposed to be haunted, are they?"

"I think the fancier the hotel the *more* haunted it is, to be honest," I counter. "Like, some shit's definitely gone down in here, you know? Fancy shit. Fancy ghost shit."

She stares at me as if she's going to let me have this one but she clearly disagrees. I mean, it's cool. Like I said before, I'm winging it.

Also it took me too long to try the door again so I have to swipe the keycard a third time to unlock and open it. But when I do--!

Nothing changes. It's still a hallway. Shit. There goes that theory.

I shrug. "Want to go in?"

"Are we allowed?" she asks.

"No clue, but that's the fun part, right?"

"...I don't think *that's* supposed to be the fun part, but, um, okay..."

We step into our potentially haunted hotel room, the entire place dim and dark, curtains drawn, the long hallway rife with pictures of all kinds of different assorted fruits. There's paintings of pomegranates, ripped open, seeds dripping with ripe red juice. There's a painting of a peach that looks remarkably like my stepsister's ass when we're going at it from behind.

Kind of into that one, actually.

There's a picture of a sexy apple, and I don't even want to explain how an apple is sexy but somehow this one's sexy. Also a sexy banana painting. Clearly there's some hardcore fucking phallic and yonic imagery going on here. Penises and vaginas for days, I swear to God, except somehow it's fine and artsy because it's fruit instead of actual penises and vaginas.

Baby Sis huddles close to me in case we're accosted by fancy ghosts and I don't have the heart to tell her I don't think I can do much against supernatural beings. I mean, fuck, I'll try my best, but it's a goddamn ghost, you know?

At the end of the hallway, a room opens up before us, still dim and dark, the curtains blocking most of the outside sunlight. An ominously glaring TV hanging on the wall to our left contains a message on the screen for us, welcoming Dave Jackson and Barbara Scott. Shadows loom through the room, eerie reflections of the items they belong to, darkness creeping across the floor, trying to make its way towards the hallway, as if waiting for us to take one more step inside so it can latch onto our feet and do something pretty fucking bad considering it's literally just shadows.

Without warning, the lights slam on, flashing bright, blinding me. I rub my eyes, adjusting to the light. When I can finally see again, Baby Sis is staring into the room like she's seen a ghost except, uh...

Holy fucking shit, what the hell is this place?

"S-sorry!" she mumbles, fingers on the lightswitch next to her. "I, um... I couldn't see, and..."

The "room," if that's what this even is, is a sprawling open-concept living area. A U-shaped sofa sits in front of the TV, forming what I guess is the living room section. In the middle of the expansive, long room is a dining table fit to seat six people; one on either end, two on either side. At the other side of the enormous room is a pool table, a bar filled with alcohol the likes of which I've never seen before, and a ridiculously large mirror adorned with wooden fruits that may or may not be phallic or yonic in nature that takes up half the wall.

Baby Sis flips another switch just because why the hell not and suddenly the curtains start to slide up, brightening the room even more with some natural sunlight. Oh, and apparently we have a goddamn fucking huge ass balcony with chairs, tables, and--

"S-sorry!" she squeaks again, snatching her fingers away from the switches to keep herself from getting into more mischief. "...Wow, is that a hot tub?" she asks, nervously pointing towards the far left end of the balcony where there is, indeed, a motherfucking hot tub.

It's on the balcony itself, overlooking the streets of Las Vegas, a prime view to relax and enjoy the sin and debauchery happening below.

"Yo, come here," I say, grabbing her hand quick and pulling her further into the room.

"H-Hunter!" she mutters. "We're going to get in trouble!"

I'm starting to realize this may actually be our hotel room. Where's the bed, though? It's not down here. And by that I mean--

In the corner of the room, near the end of the balcony with the hot tub, there's a slightly hidden set of stairs leading to a loft-style overhang above us. I get Baby Sis to the stairs first and foremost, then I lift her up into my arms, drape her over my shoulder like I do this all the time. I kind of do it more than I've ever done it before. What can I say? She's fun to carry around. She does this flailing kick and shriek thing and it's cute as hell, man.

She never flails or kicks *too* hard. That's important. If she did, I'd probably drop her on accident. She does it just enough to express her frustration with me, you know, carrying her around like a caveman, but I'm pretty sure she's into it.

Anyways, I drag her sexy fucking ass upstairs, give her butt a good smack at the top for good luck, and promptly put her back on her feet in our brand new luxury bedroom.

Fuck yeah, this place is rad as hell.

"*Excuse* me," she says, hands in her hips, shyly glaring at me. "You aren't a caveman and I'm not a sack of potatoes."

"Are you sure I'm not a caveman?" I ask, just in case.

"Yes," she says, faster than necessary.

"I was actually thinking you're more like my hot cavewoman babe instead of a sack of potatoes, too," I add. "Does that help?"

"A little bit but I don't want to admit it," she says, blushing softly.

It's just a tiny blush. Nowhere near what I know I can get out of her. Still, I like it, though. Her cheeks are perfect and I want to kiss the fuck out them right now, not least because the bed behind her looks perfect for what we're going to do later. Or not. Let's just do it now. And later. Both. Fuck me, man.

Baby Sis finally turns around because I'm openly staring at our hotel bed.

And, uh, yeah...

Look, it's *also* pomegranate shaped, and by that I mean it's massive and round. I think it's bigger than a king-sized bed but who even knows. The sheets are red silk and the blankets are crushed red velvet, with the curved wooden headboard along the back rising up, edges decorated like the skin of a pomegranate that's been sliced open. The pillows are a deep, dark red, almost black but not quite.

There's also a note near the pillows with a remote control next to it.

"...We need to leave," Baby Sis says after she takes a long hard look at our bed for the weekend. "I think we're in the wrong room? Oh gosh, someone's going to be mad. They're going to find us in their room and they're going to--"

"Dude, relax," I tell her. "Our names were on the TV downstairs. It's definitely our room."

"Those were our parents' names, though," she points out.

"...Which is how we know this is our room," I continue. "Because we pretended to be them to check in, remember?"

"Oh, right. Um, I'm still confused about that. I know *why* we needed to do it then, but, um... we don't have to do it anymore, right?"

"Nah, we're good," I say, a little too soon.

I check the note on the bed and it's addressed to our parents. Or us. Same thing.

Anyways, it says:

. . .

"Mr. Jackson and Ms. Scott,

We welcome you to the Metropolitan Signature hotel for the luxury weekend getaway of your dreams! As our jackpot winners, we want to make your stay extra special. If there's anything you need, please call down to the front desk and we'll arrange delivery for you. On top of that, as per the conditions of your prize, we've created an itinerary for your stay. Your personal butler will arrive shortly to cater to your every need and desire.

Rest assured, the Pomegranate Suite is the absolute epitome of opulence, as you'll soon find out. Many refer to it as our honeymoon suite, but it's so much more. This is where dreams are not only created, but experienced in their entirety. To that end, please allow me to inform you of a few of the benefits to your room:

Your PERFECT CIRCLE bed is fitted with state of the art controls unlike anything you've ever seen before. Using the remote control, you can customize the bed as you see fit, to suit any and all of your needs. The bed has a massage function, a sinful seduction mode, and many of our guests enjoy the TOURNER setting which slowly rotates the bed in a constant 360° circle.

The hot tub is perfect for relaxing morning breaks or a late evening affair. While we do request you "keep it clean" as it were, we've provided special condoms intended for this very purpose if you're feeling wild and adventurous. Anything goes in the Pomegranate Suite. If you do decide to use the hot tub for adventurous purposes, please leave the associated placard on the side so your butler can arrange the correct cleaning routine during our daily hot tub maintenance. This is mandatory and occurs at 2PM every day. Please be aware of this so you can plan for it.

Last but not least, as a special guest of the Metropolitan, we invite you to dine in our various hotel fine dining establishments as our honored guests. You absolutely MUST try the Chef's Kiss menu. It's the perfect experience to start off a night of classy sin and sophisticated debauchery.

Please note: dining in our various restaurants at certain times is *a necessary condition of your luxury weekend stay. Your butler will inform you of these specific requirements.*

If there's anything else you need, please say the word. If needed, I can be contacted directly at the number below. I hope we can make your stay with us memorable and special.

Thank you, now, as always,

~ Anthony Montcalm

General Manager, Metropolitan Hotel (A Harriott Signature Hotel)"

"Dude," I say to Baby Sis immediately after reading the letter.

"Dude?" she says, but I don't think we're duding about the same thing right now.

"Want to try the bed?"

"Kind of?" she answers, blushing hard.

That's pretty much all I need in order to lift her ass up again, toss her onto the fine velvety blankets, and--

We don't get far. I have one shoe off and she's struggling to untie hers because they're too tight to pull off easily. At about the same time that I start to pull my sock off, a motherfucking doorbell rings, jingling through the entire suite.

"...Was that a doorbell?" Baby Sis asks, holding the end of her shoelace, ready to pull so she can finally start to get undressed. Or, you know, at least take her shoes off.

"Yeah," I say, nodding.

We just kind of sit there for way longer than we should, trying to figure out what the hell a doorbell in a hotel room even means?

After about ten seconds it rings again.

As much as I hate to say it, testing out the sinful seduction mode on this bed is gonna have to wait.

Baby Sis pouts as I pull her up off the bed, both of us wearing one shoe as we head downstairs to see what's up.

CHARLOTTE

Apparently fancy hotel luxury suites have doorbells? Or this one does. Which, um... yes, so…

Hunter and I head downstairs, each of us wearing a single shoe. Different shoes. We're not wearing the same shoe with both our feet in it. I have mine on and he has his on and we're both missing one and I don't know if this is actually important or relevant to the doorbell but maybe?

Anyways, we hurry to the door because the person outside is very insistently ringing the doorbell every ten seconds .

"C-coming!" I shout out in case that helps. "We were, um... shoes?"

Hunter stops in his tracks and I stop too because now he's staring at me and I don't know why.

He shakes his head. "Dude. Really?"

I awkwardly wave my partially bare foot at him. It still has a sock, but the shoe's definitely missing. In case he doesn't understand, I tap my sock-covered toes against his, which also has a sock on it.

He stares at my foot while I belatedly realize I'm playing footsie with him. As soon as I realize what I'm doing, my cheeks turn cherry red.

"I don't mean to alarm you," a female voice informs us from the corridor. "But I really can stand out here all day. I have nothing else to do."

She doesn't sound mad or annoyed or, um... anything, really. It's a very matter-of-fact statement and I don't think

I've ever heard anyone say something like that in quite that way before.

While Hunter's staring at my foot, I scamper to the door, pull the handle down, and swing it inwards.

Standing outside is an immaculately dressed woman with short-cropped strawberry blonde hair ending in curls. She's wearing a crisp blue velvet suit with clean white gloves and shiny white leather shoes. A fashionable scarf's wrapped around her neck and tucked into the front of her suit jacket, almost like a tie except, um... it's a scarf? A shimmering silver rectangular button pinned to the left side of her jacket indicates she's the Pomegranate Suite Butler.

"Hello," she says, curt. "Mr. Jackson and Ms. Scott, I presume? My name is Francoise and I'll be taking care of your every need this weekend. It's a pleasure to make your acquaintance."

Hunter steps next to me in the doorway, sizing up the woman standing outside. She's not very tall but she looks really formidable. I wouldn't want to, um... I mean, I wouldn't want to start a fight with *anyone,* but I definitely wouldn't want to fight her? I don't even know how to fight. But I'm sure she'd be willing to have a polite chat with me about our differences if it came to that, too. She seems like that kind of woman.

"Uh, hey?" Hunter says. "You're a woman."

"Yes, I am," Francoise replies, as if none of this bothers her in the least. "Do you have any other questions for me?"

"Are you really our butler?" I ask, because I feel like we're supposed to ask things and it's the first thing I can think of.

"Yes, I am," Francoise answers, curt and to the point. "As I mentioned, I'm here to attend to your every need this weekend."

"I don't want to be a dick, but what does that even mean?" Hunter asks.

I'm glad he asked because I have no idea either.

Francoise nods, clearly very ready for this. She clears her throat and begins with:

"If you require anything, I will fetch it immediately, whatever it may be. Mind, you may need to pay for it, but my time and service are already paid for by the hotel. If you have any questions, I'm happy to answer them. I can perform laundry duties, which are covered by your room incidentals. I can order room service, make reservations at any restaurant within fifty miles of the Greater Las Vegas area with little to no notice. I fancy myself an avid jigsaw puzzle solver. I can mix drinks using the liquors present in the bar in your room. I'm not a professional baker by any means, but I dabble in cakes and cookies on occasion. I can find out the name of a song if you can hum me a few bars. I've lived in Las Vegas for the past ten years and will be able to assist you with any touring, clubbing, dancing, events, or other similar requests."

I nod along as if this is a regular thing to do when someone is telling you all this.

"And, last but not least," Francoise says, taking a modest breath before continuing. "While Las Vegas is known as the City of Sin, please do recognize that prostitution is illegal within the city limits. If you wish to enjoy that particular experience, I'm happy to assist and can drive you to a legal brothel outside the city limits. While I'd prefer you choose a professional working girl, of which I know many I can recommend, if the price is right, well, what can I say? I'm available."

She says that last part with a sly smirk and a silly wink and I have no idea if she's serious.

"Wait, um, there's actually prostitutes?" I ask.

"Dude..." Hunter says, duding me again.

"What!" I mumble. "I just, um... I didn't know that was real?"

"It's definitely real, Ms. Scott," Francoise informs me,

infinitely curt. "Is it Ms. Scott, by the way? Mrs. perhaps? Or do you prefer your husband's name? Ms. or Mrs. Jackson?"

"Um, you can call me Charlotte if you want to?"

"Dude!" Hunter says, doing it again!

What the heck, Hunter. I don't even know why you're so--

Oh, wait. I get it now... Shoot, I screwed up, didn't I?

Before I make this worse, Hunter promptly closes the door, leaving Francoise standing outside in the hallway. He drags me far enough away from the door that I don't think she can hear us anymore but I don't actually know if she can.

And then, hasty, he whispers, "I don't know if you remember, but we're supposed to be our parents for the weekend according to the hotel, right?"

"...I did remember that just now, yes," I say, nervously nodding. "Um... I... I don't know if I can do it, Hunter! I thought we only had to do it at the front desk?"

"Yeah, same, but she works for the hotel, so..."

"She seems nice?"

"You think so? She seems kind of weird to me."

"I can hear you perfectly, by the way," Francoise says, short and simple.

"Shoot," I mumble

"Uh, yeah..." Hunter says.

Hunter and I head back to the door and slowly open it a second time. Francoise's standing outside in the exact same position as before, hands at her side, short strawberry curls still in the exact same spot. She's very good at this, if this is a butler thing, which, um... I don't know if it is but whatever it is she's very good at it.

"May I inquire as to *who* you actually are?" she asks, eyes narrowed.

"No?" I say, hoping that works.

"Very well," she says. "I'll inform the front desk there's been a mistake. Please wait here. If we need to forcibly remove you from the premises, please rest assured we have a rear entrance that allows for discretion. We would never remove unwelcome guests using the front entrance. It's gauche and would cause an unnecessary scene."

"Shit, uh, wait!" Hunter says as Francoise turns on a dime, her white leather shoes perfectly pivoting on the corridor carpeting.

She hesitates before taking a step, but the way she's standing makes it clear she could do it at any moment.

"Yes?" she asks, head cocked slightly to the side, eyes on Hunter.

"Look, can we do this inside?" he asks.

"So you can potentially restrain me, kidnap me, or do any other number of untold unmentionables to my person?" she asks, one brow raised very very high. "No. Thank you."

"She has a point?" I say to Hunter. "I, um... I don't think I'd come inside if I were her, either."

"Thank you, Ms. Scott," Francoise says with a wry smile. "If that's your name."

"Um, it is..." I mumble. "And... no...?"

Hunter sighs and I don't know what we're sighing about but I try to sigh along with him. I'm not good at it. Mostly I'm nervous and now my stomach hurts and I just want to come clean because I'm really bad at lying so, um...

"Our... our parents won the jackpot prize and they wanted to give it to us and we know it's against the rules but, um... please don't tell anyone?"

"Can you explain that bit about being booted out through the back again?" Hunter asks. "Do you think it's possible for us to just, you know, *not* do that and leave on our own instead?"

"H-Hunter!" I say, trying not to laugh. "Maybe, um... maybe we can..."

I probably shouldn't laugh because we're seriously about to get kicked out, aren't we?

"I accept your request to come in now," Francoise informs

us, stepping through the doorway and past us. "Let's discuss a mutually beneficial working arrangement, shall we?"

I have no idea what that means. I don't think Hunter does, either. He looks at me and I look at him as Francoise strides down the front hall to the living room with purpose and confidence.

Hunter shrugs. I close the door. We all head to the couch to, um... talk, or...

Are we getting kicked out already? I really wanted to see the bed spin in a circle first.

HUNTER

Look, was this a bad idea? Yes, yes it was.

It's not even that it was *bad.* The idea was fine. But Baby Sis is a terrible liar so I don't know why anyone expected her to be able to pull this off. Like, out of everyone I know, she's the last person I'd ask to do something like this.

Uh, besides Teddy. I wouldn't ask Teddy, either. He'd be worse at this than Baby Sis and I don't even know how.

Anyways, Francoise sits primly on our couch, somehow looking feminine and masculine at the same time. She's clearly attractive, but I don't know if she's attractive in a feminine or masculine way if that even makes sense? Like, uh... she's very atypical is all I'm going to say. She looks like she could judo toss your ass on the ground if you got out of line but also she'd probably give you the best blowjob in the world if you were looking for that, which I'm not, because I have a girlfriend, thanks.

Neither of those things is decidedly feminine or masculine, are they? Fuck. That's what's so confusing to me right now.

Right, so--

"As I understand it, you're the son and daughter of Mr.

Jackson and Ms. Scott, the winners of the slot machine jackpot prize?" Francoise asks, straightforward.

"Um, yes," Baby Sis instantly answers, happy not to have to lie her ass off anymore.

"Sort of," I say, clarifying further. "It's my dad and her mom, but it's not my mom or her dad?"

"Step," Baby Sis says, nodding nervously.

"You're stepsiblings?" Francoise asks. "Hmm. I would've sworn you were intimate. You have the body language of lovers who have been... hold on, let me think... not *too* long. Perhaps a few months now?"

"Um... yes..." Baby Sis says, still failing so fucking hard.

Like, dude, come on. I know you're bad at this, but you don't have to instantly tell the truth all the time, either?

"Interesting," Francoise says, smirking. "Continue."

"No offense but what are we continuing exactly?" I ask. "I thought you were kicking us out?"

"As far as I can ascertain, you're not doing anything otherwise illegal, though you are circumventing the rules set forth by the jackpot prize commission. Thankfully for you, that's none of my business. If you are who you say you are, I have no reason to interfere. I'm in the service of Mr. Jackson and Ms. Scott this weekend, and if they opted to allow their son and daughter to stay in their place, well..."

"Does this mean I get to see how the bed works? I was really excited to see it spin," Baby Sis says, completely missing every and any point ever.

"It's fun. Shall I show you?" Francoise asks.

"Yo!" I say, stopping the girls before they go way too fucking far here. "Hold up. How do you know we are who we say we are?"

"Good point," Francoise says with a slight nod. "I don't. Let's rectify that. IDs please. Real ones. Now that you've told me the truth, let's not play coy."

"Okay," Baby Sis says, instantly reaching into her pocket to find her license. She hands it over without a second thought.

"Dude!" I say.

"What!" she says back. "I'm *trying*, Hunter..."

"I see why you want to be called Charlotte now, Ms. Scott," Francoise says after inspecting my stepsister's ID and handing it back. "Shall I call you Ms. Scott in the presence of the other hotel staff?"

"Um, yes?"

Holy fucking shit what the fuck is happening.

Grunting and really fucking pissed off about it, I shove my fist into my pocket, pull out my wallet, rip out my real drivers license, and thrust it at the Pomegranate Suite butler.

"Here," I say. "Happy?"

She inspects it, nods, and hands it back. "Mr. Jackson," she says. "Would you prefer Hunter in private and Mr. Jackson in front of other hotel staff, as well?"

"Actually yeah that would be great if you don't mind?" I say, because I'm done. Just gonna go with whatever, I guess.

"Very well. Also, as I've now confirmed, you're both under the legal drinking age. So, as to protect the hotel from any potential indemnity, I must insist on removing the alcohol from your room."

"Okay," Baby Sis says.

"I mean, I guess that's fine?" I say with a shrug. "Wasn't planning on drinking it anyways."

"I'm glad we could come to an understanding," Francoise says with a subtle smile. "What you do outside the hotel is none of my business, so please continue your weekend however you planned to otherwise."

"Understood," Baby Sis says, nodding slightly, totally getting into it now.

"Dude," I say, rolling my eyes at her.

"Um, can we see the bed spin now?" she asks.

"Yeah, sure, why not."

"A wonderful choice, Charlotte!" Francoise informs her. "I can make you acquainted with all the modes and functions of your luxury PERFECT CIRCLE bed, of which there are many. I understand the general manager left you a note regarding that? It's more fun to see it in action, though. Now, if you'll come with me I would be happy to--"

Yeah. It's exactly what it sounds like. Our private butler shows us how our fancy ass circle bed works.

I wish it wasn't as cool as it is in action but holy fucking shit it's awesome.

PRETENDING FOR THE WEEKEND

Episode 186

CHARLOTTE

The ceiling above me slowly spins as I lay in the middle of the PERFECT CIRCLE bed in the upstairs loft of the Pomegranate Suite at the Metropolitan Signature hotel.

Technically I'm spinning but, um... shhhhh.

Anyways--

Hunter didn't want to spin. He's fine just watching me spin, and I'm fine with spinning? I think that's how relationships are sometimes. One person is the doer and the other person is the, um... the person having things done to them...

I belatedly realize this is probably really applicable for steamy possibilities and also I should consider writing this down in my notebook for future romance steamy scene writing ideas. It's so obvious now that I think about it and I don't know why I didn't think about it before now?

"I don't want to be an asshole," Hunter says, standing on one side of the bed while Francoise mans the remote on the other side. "But what's the point of having a spinning bed? Like, why would anyone ever want their bed to spin?"

"It's kind of fun?" I say while spinning. I reach my hands up on the bed as I spin a slow circle near Hunter, wiggling my fingers to try and reach for him. I don't quite make it before I'm slowly spinning away again.

"The TOURNER function, as it's officially referred to, is intended to offer you the opportunity to have whatever view you wish to have of your room at any time," Francoise informs him, sounding like an infomercial operator. "While you can make the bed spin on its own, like so, you can *also* rotate the headboard if you wish, meaning you could, for example, turn the entire bed so it faces the bathroom."

"Or the wall," Hunter points out. "Which I really don't understand. Also... again... no offense, not trying to be an asshole here, but why would I want to rotate the bed to face the bathroom."

"While I can't speak for *everyone*," Francoise says, nodding crisply. "Many individuals find that function appealing if only for the fact that the bathroom in the Pomegranate Suite is outfitted with a luxury, state of the art bathtub, which easily fits two people, and may be something many wish to enjoy before immediately absconding to the bed afterwards. Also, if you adjust the bed as such, *just so,* the person currently occupying the bed can see into the bathroom straight to the bathtub, which may be appealing depending on certain circumstances."

Francoise points me towards the bathroom to showcase how this works. Granted, the, um... the bathroom light is off and I can't see much of anything but I think I can vaguely make out the edge of a bathtub sitting within view?

"Okay, so you're saying if I were to, say, lay in bed, and Baby Sis wanted to screw with me, she could steal the remote, set herself up with a sexy bubble bath, and then point me right at her so I could see her doing sexy bubble bath things in the bathroom?" Hunter says, deciding the TOURNER feature is, in fact, potentially useful. "Should've led with that one."

"H-Hunter!" I squeak, no longer spinning. I mumble and blush and scurry up and off the bed to, um... I'm just going to hide somewhere for a second but I don't know where yet.

Also Francoise ignores all that and focuses on something else he said instead.

"*Baby Sis?*" she asks, one neat eyebrow raised impeccably high.

"Ummmmmmm..." I mumble, because I'm not the one who needs to explain this. Hunter said it. He can do it.

"Yeah, uh... yeah..." he mutters. "Fuck. Alright, look, before we were, uh... you know... we were... you know, instead, and..."

"No," our butler informs us. "I have no idea what any of that means."

"Um, when H-Hunter became my stepbrother he, um... he wanted to tease me a lot? And he still kind of does but it's not so bad. It's kind of nice? I... shouldn't have said that out loud. D-don't tease me too much, Hunter!" I stammer, trying to explain.

"Look, I started calling her Baby Sis because it was funny and I can't stop now, because she makes me do it, so there you go."

"I don't *make* you do it!" I protest. "I mean, I like it, but I don't *make* you do it..."

"Strange, but understandable," Francoise says. "Shall I continue with the demonstration?"

"Yes, please," I say, excited, clapping my hands together.

Next up is apparently the Sinful Seduction feature, which is actually just a fancy way of saying the bed is counter-reactive. What this apparently means, because I have no idea at first, is that, um... if you set it to Sinful Seduction mode, any impact against the bed at a certain force will be countered by a similarly impactful counter-force.

Basically, um...

If we're having sex and it's regular and I'm laying on the bed and Hunter's pressed above me, thrusting into me, um... as we do, if we're *really* going at a good speed and pace, the bed will, um... assist, by, you know...

Pushing back?

"I don't have personal experience with this mode, but I've been told it's similar to making love on an ocean wave," Francoise says with a simple nod.

"...Is that good or bad?" I ask, confused.

Francoise shrugs and smirks, enigmatic. "I suppose you can find out for yourself sometime?"

Hunter looks like he's ready to kick her out of our room and see for himself right here and now and I'm definitely interested except at the worst possible moment my phone starts to ring.

I hear it but it's far away sounding and I belatedly realize I left it downstairs. The only person who would be calling me right now is my mom, so...

"S-sorry!" I squeak, scrambling over to the stairs, hurrying down, grabbing my phone, answering it fast, and then running back up.

I don't know why I run back upstairs. I'm not paying attention at the moment. In my mad dash to answer my mom's call, I accidentally answer on speakerphone, which is very awkward and embarrassing for a soon-to-be revealed reason.

"Hi, um, mom," I mumble, holding the phone to my ear.

"Baby!" my mom says, screaming through my phone, her voice blasting through the room, deafening me. "Tell me *everything!* How is it? Is it amazing? I bet it's amazing."

"Um, it's amazing," I say, frantically dragging the phone away from my ear. Instead of turning off speakerphone, I just kind of hold my phone in front of me instead. "The bed spins."

"It spins?" my mom asks. "How cool! Why, though?"

"I guess so you can have a view of the bathtub if you want?"

"Huh! I can think of a few uses for that. Too bad me and your new stepdad couldn't try it out. Ha! Not that you and Hunter will be doing the same thing, but let me know how it looks? Take pictures!"

...I'm very glad this isn't a video call at the moment because my cheeks hurt from blushing...

I kind of want to try the spinning bathtub thing with Hunter later? If, um... if he wants to, that is...

"Did you check in alright?" my mom asks. "You didn't have any trouble, did you? I know you're not good at making up stories, but what's the harm, right? No one found out, did they?"

"Ummmmm..." I murmur.

"Ms. Scott," Francoise says, inserting herself into the conversation. "Your daughter and stepson have informed me of the situation. As your personal butler for this weekend, am I to understand that you wish for me to service them?"

"Oh my gosh I'm on speakerphone!" my mom says, both surprised and elated. "Wait, who's that? Did the hotel send up an escort? That's so funny!"

"As I just said, I'm a butler, ma'am," Francoise says. "Pardon my previous terminology. I'm not currently authorized to provide the service you just mentioned."

"Is she a stripper?" my mom asks, not really getting it. "Did they send up a stripper?"

"Mom, she's a butler," I say. "She's here to, um... to butler?"

...Is that what butlers do? I really hope so...

"Wait, seriously? So she works for the hotel? Shoot. Are you two getting kicked out?" my mom asks.

"*Ms. Scott,*" Francoise says, clearing her throat and trying again. "If you could please give me verbal indication that it's you and your husband's desire that I make certain your daughter and stepson have an appropriately perfect weekend together, I believe we can forego telling the hotel of any other potential indiscretions."

"She sounds cute. Hunter! Is Hunter there, baby? Hunter, is the butler cute?"

"Mom!" I say, frantic.

I wish the bed had a spot underneath it where I could hide, except it doesn't. The frame goes all the way to the floor. It's impossible.

"She's, uh... I mean, I guess she's cute?" Hunter offers, staring at me as if to ask why he's even answering her.

"I do my best to maintain a pleasing physical appearance," Francoise informs us with pure professionalism. "*Now,* ma'am..."

"Well, shoot, of course you can take care of my babies!" my mom says, giddy. "They're not in trouble, right? Let me know if you need me to bail them out of jail?"

"Mom..." I murmur, flat.

I look at Hunter, trying to ask him with my eyes if I can hang up now, but I don't think I can. He sighs and shakes his head and I don't know if he understands what I mean but it's fine.

"I will most certainly take care of your babies," Francoise lets her know. "Unfortunately, as per the contractual obligations involved in your jackpot prize, Hunter and Charlotte will need to pretend to be husband and wife in public for the duration of their stay, at least while at the Metropolitan hotel."

"Aww, how fun!" my mom says, absolutely loving the idea for some reason. "They get along so well already. Almost like they're an old married couple! Ha. They're just so good together, am I right? I'm sure you know what I mean even if you only just met them. It's really nice. What's your name again? Sorry, I didn't catch it earlier."

"Francoise, Ms. Scott," she says, matter-of-fact.

"Such a pretty name!" my mom tells her. "Well, Francoise, as you may have noticed, my baby and my new baby just get along so well, don't they? Baby. Charlotte, I mean. That baby. I know it's kind of different or maybe weird pretending Hunter's your husband but you can do it! I believe in you. Just don't make it too real, you know? Joking! But seriously, don't come back pregnant. That's way too real. Joking again! But not actually? I mean, you have an IUD now so you should be fine and can't get pregnant, but that's, well... you know, that's not what I meant. Baby, it's just pretend, that's all."

Hunter and I have been testing the limits of my IUD for awhile now and so far no babies have happened so I think we're fine on that front.

...We haven't been pretending to be husband and wife, but we've definitely been, um... *not* pretending about the marital bed aspects if we *were* pretending to be husband and wife, so...

I'm not saying any of this out loud to my mother, ever, nope, not a chance.

"I just wanted to check in and make sure you two got there safe," my mom adds. "Sorry about the fake marriage stuff! I know you two get along so well. I didn't mean to make it awkward between you two. You're just really good friends, right? I love that about you two. It's like you're a real brother and sister now and that's just really nice. It's so nice, babies! Francoise, isn't that nice? Please don't get the wrong idea about them. Charlotte's dating this nice boy named Teddy. He's Hunter's best friend. And Hunter's dating Teddy's sister. It's actually super sweet. I just love it. Anyways! Okay bye, babies! Bye Charlotte! Bye Hunter! Bye Francoise!"

"B-bye Mom..." I mumble. It's the only thing I can manage to say at the moment.

"Farewell, Ms. Scott," Francoise says, perfectly polite.

"Uh, yeah," Hunter grunts.

My mom's kind of living in her own world though so she just sort of hangs up and that's it.

I hold my phone out in front of me still, not sure what to do with it, really regretting the fact that I accidentally put it on speakerphone and we ended up having that conversation.

"Is it correct for me to assume your mother doesn't know of the less-than-friendly aspects of your relationship?" Francoise asks us.

"Uh, yeah..." Hunter grunts again.

"Nope..." I mumble, agreeing.

"May I ask if this is because she wouldn't agree with it?" Francoise asks.

"...I don't actually know?" I answer, unsure. "Um... is it bad? I don't know if it's bad."

"Alright, look," Hunter says, taking charge. "It's my fault. We should've told our parents a long time ago. Or, uh... like, a month or two ago at least. But I asked Baby Sis to hold off because I didn't want to fuck anything up, and also, it's a really fucked up situation in the first place, so..."

"Um, both our parents are married," I explain to our butler. "My mom is married to Hunter's dad and Hunter's mom is married to my dad?"

Francoise raises both of her neatly manicured eyebrows now, clearly impressed at our special brand of forbidden romance.

"Anyways, long story short, I think we can probably pretend to be husband and wife this weekend?" Hunter adds.

"Please don't make me pretend to be my mom!" I mutter.

"There's one other option," Francoise says, smiling politely

"Uh, no there's not," Hunter says.

"Wait, there is?" I ask, hopeful.

"You *are* Ms. Scott, are you not?" Francoise points out. "Just not *the* Ms. Scott that the hotel thinks you are."

"...Yes...?"

"And you're already in an otherwise loving and presumably intimate relationship?" Francoise continues. "I don't mean to assume or imply anything, but if that's the case, you two should easily be able to pass as romantically involved, whatever the actual terms of your relationship are. So..."

Hunter and I stare at her, and I don't think either of us gets it yet so she keeps going.

"Do what you already do, don't hide the kisses, the hand holding, whatever else you've both been doing in private, and act, for all intents and purposes, as if you're in a relationship, without thinking about it as anything else. Let others assume you're married and it should be easy to pull off."

I blink and look over at Hunter and he blinks and looks back at me, and, um...

"Sounds kind of nice?" Hunter says.

"Okay," I agree, smiling bright.

"Cool. Want to be my pretend wife for the weekend?" he asks with a smirk.

"Yes, please!" I say, really excited about it now.

I don't think I can pull off pretending to be my mom, but I'm positive I can easily pretend to be in love with Hunter.

Um, I already am, so...

It sounds so easy when we say it like that in our hotel room.

Unfortunately, later, um... it's not as easy as I thought...?

(About thirty minutes later, as part of the mandatory jackpot prize experience...)

I don't know why I agreed to any of this and I wish I could explain how awkward and embarrassing it is, but I can't. Even *trying* to explain it is embarrassing.

I'm standing in the Nightfall Cocktail Bar in the Metropolitan Signature hotel next to this very odd, dusky blue couch. It's a circle, for one. I've never seen a circle couch before. I wonder if that's a theme for the hotel? Lots of circle things. Ummm, first the bed and now the couch? I don't know.

The couch is odd enough on its own but it's also fitted around a pillar, which has the same dusky blue material riding up it as the couch. So basically it's a pillar, but also a couch? You can't sit on the pillar, though.

To be fair, it's a really nice couch and the material feels so soft and smooth and I'd love to sit on it right about now but I'm having some personal issues and I'm struggling enough as it is so, um... no thank you...

I clench my legs together, thighs tight, knees pressed close, as I stand next to the couch, waiting for Hunter to get back, hoping he doesn't get any terrible horrible awful ideas while he's gone, because please just don't, Hunter!

This was a bad idea. Really bad. I thought it'd be fun. I don't know why. I thought I could handle it, because, um... I didn't realize how intense it would feel?

It's the moving part. Literally just moving makes me--

BZZZZZZT!

I open my mouth and hold back a gasp, trying to relax, to act like nothing's going on. It is, though. I mean, it was. It was quick, sudden, and then it stopped, so that's good, but it's not *good* good if that makes sense?

Thankfully Francoise appears shortly after with a drink for me. She carries it on a silver platter, holding it up neatly, letting me take the cocktail glass from the center of the tray at my leisure.

I, um... I nervously reach my hand out to grab the stem of the glass, hoping beyond hope nothing happens within the fraction of a second it takes for me to--

I pause, nervous, my fingers nearly within reach of the stem. Francoise watches me with a cool, calculated, slightly critical gaze, as if she's unsure what I'm doing but professional protocol dictates she shouldn't say anything about it, either.

When nothing happens after a few seconds, I quickly grab the glass, holding it tight to my chest.

"A mocktail, obviously," Francoise informs me. "This is a non-alcoholic version of one of our mixologist's most popular concoctions, the *Plus Ultra,* named after the famed flying boat, an aircraft from the 1920s that completed the first transatlantic flight from Spain to South America. Please take note of the shimmering quality of the indigo flecks within the glass combined with streaks of silvery grey. The taste is divine and combines flavors of banana, citrus, and a dash of a traditional Chinese five spice blend. This gives the beverage a hint of spicy sweetness in the form of star anise, cinnamon, and that lovely bite of cloves and peppercorn, tempered slightly by the fennel. It is meant to be savored as a special indulgence, Ms. Scott."

She says all of this and I hear most of it except right at the end the *BZZZZZT!* happens again and the only way I can think to hide my obvious reaction is to, um... shove the edge of the glass close to my lips as I open my mouth in yet another gasp.

I don't sip at first. I can't. I can smell the drink and I think that makes it even worse. If this is an aphrodisiac, um... it's a good one. I don't think it's supposed to be, though. That's another issue entirely.

Right as Francoise finishes explaining the flavor profile to me I take a sip and try and calm down once the buzzing stops.

I don't mean to but after I taste the drink and swallow my small mouthful, I let out a gasp of a moan.

It's, um... yup...

"That's not the usual reaction guests have after tasting that particular drink, but I daresay it's fitting," my butler for the weekend says with a sliver of a smirk.

"Um, it's... it's very g-good..." I mumble, fidgeting side to side, knowing full well I'll never get used to this.

We have to stay here for a full hour, though. Ugh. *How?*

...Please stop teasing me Hunter...

In case none of this makes sense yet--

(About thirty minutes earlier, back in the Pomegranate Suite...)

"Your itinerary for today as special guests is somewhat packed earlier on," Francoise informs us after we finish the speakerphone chat with my mom. "I would've discussed this with you sooner, but, well, we all know how that went. At any rate, you're expected to attend the daily cocktail hour at the Nightfall Cocktail Bar on the fifth floor in approximately half an hour. I'll leave you to it until then. Please change into something casual yet suitable. A dress is fine, Charlotte. For you, Hunter, I'd recommend a nice pair of slacks, though denim is also acceptable, and a buttondown shirt. Casual or semi-casual footwear is appropriate. Think of it as a meet and greet between guests in a cool and contemporary setting."

This is what Francoise said right before leaving me and Hunter alone in the Pomegranate Suite.

"So," Hunter says after the door automatically swings closed behind her.

"Ummmm?" I answer, because the look in his eyes is

clearly indicative of something that we definitely don't have time to do in thirty minutes if we still want to get ready.

"Look, I know we don't have time right now," he says.

"Oh, good," I add, breathing a minor sigh of relief. "Umm... it's not that I don't *want* to..." I add, just in case.

Because I really really do and I want him to know that...

"Yeah, I get it..." Hunter says, but for some reason that same look is still in his eyes and I have no idea what it means.

"C-can you please stop looking at me like that?" I mumble. "It's, um... *why!*"

Hunter laughs and pulls me tight, hugging me instead of kissing me and having his way with me. So I think we're on the same page? I feel like I would really struggle to stop him from having his way with me if he started having his way with me because I want him to have his way with me too and if we had more time I'd also want to have my way with him, but, um, we just don't, you know?

It's very sad, honestly.

"I know we don't have time for everything we talked about doing when we got here, but maybe we could try something?" he asks.

I realize this a lot later but these are very dangerous words and alarm bells should've been ringing in my head as soon as I heard them. They didn't, though. I was naive and innocent. I, um... I mean, really though, I only just started reading the steamy scenes in romance novels a couple months ago and I only started doing, um... anything, really, with just myself or with Hunter, like... not even a couple months ago, so...

Look, this all sounded like a great idea at the time and it seemed fun and silly and flirty and exciting because I didn't realize how terribly wrong it could go, so, um...

S-sorry! I just wanted to have fun with my boyfriend and pretend husband for the weekend...

"You want to try out some of the toys we brought?" Hunter asks, sinfully seductive, whispering the words to me, sending them straight to the primed and ready pleasure centers percolating in the deepest recesses of my brain.

"...H-Hunter..." I mumble, trying to stay strong. You can do this, Charlotte! It's fine. It's, um... "We... we don't have time..."

"Nah, we do for this," he says with absolute confidence. "What I was thinking is--"

Again, I want to point out that at the time it seemed fun and flirty and sexy and...

But basically this is how I ended up naked on our circle bed while Hunter teased me into seriously wet arousal. He took out the toys in question, the ones I fully agreed to try out after he explained his plan. I, um... I consented to this...

Anyways, yes.

Hunter pries my thighs apart, staring down at my glistening wet kitty, my entire core on high alert, ready and waiting to be satisfied and fulfilled. I clench my eyes shut, not really knowing exactly what's going to happen or how it's going to feel but, um... I'm ready!

...I think I'm ready but honestly I don't even know...

He teases his tongue up along my arousal slick slit, right between my lower lips, tasting my wetness. I shiver and gasp and right as I'm getting used to the sensation, he gets to the top, to my, um... my pearl, and as soon as he slowly, sensually licks a circle around it I'm basically done for. I gasp and let out a moan and my hips start to wriggle, trying to rise up to meet his face.

He pulls away, smirking at me from between my legs. When I open my eyes to complain with a pout, just that, um... I don't know if it'll work but I'm going to give him a really pouty look, because. Anyways, that doesn't work so well because as soon as I open my eyes he slides one finger up and down my wetness and when he's gathered enough to make quick work of me, he does that. Just, um... inside, you know? And up. *Curled.*

He pushes his middle finger in me and I gasp and buck

and lift my hips up again but this time he's ready for it. He pushes me back down, the palm of his free hand pressing against my lower stomach. He pins me to the bed, teasing me with one finger, working me up for the plan to come.

This wasn't even the plan! I *wish* this was the plan. I wouldn't *mind* if it was the plan. But it's not.

The plan is--

Hunter pulls his finger out and I desperately want him to keep going but he isn't doing that anymore. Slow, meticulous, making me watch his every move, he takes our small bottle of water-based lube that's just sitting on the side of the bed, waiting to be used. Opening the top, he squirts some in the palm of one hand. With the other hand, he picks up the imminent means of my lust-driven demise.

It's, um... it's the ben wa balls from my toy box that Angela and Clarissa sent me and I've heard things about them, *really good things*, so, um...

Rolling the weighted balls in his palm, covering them in slick lubricant, he grins at me as I watch him, this giddy, overeager excited smile slowly spreading across my face. I, um... I just get really excited when we try new things because maybe it'll give me good ideas for future steamy scenes I'm writing in my romance stories?

Huntley and Chantel's story is almost done, but I have an idea for another one after that and--

Hunter presses the curve of the first ball between my lower lips. It's cool to the touch, the lube not as warm as Hunter's finger, but it heats up fast.

Slow, careful, he pushes the ball inside me, my body resisting slightly at first, unsure about this new, cool sensation. And then, um...

Pop?

It's in.

The second ball follows and they both just kind of easily fit inside me and that's it. That's it at first, anyways. I feel them, feel the sensation of, um... not being *entirely* full, but I can clearly feel them in there, you know?

The only indicator that I have anything inside me is the looped string attached to the end of the second ball, which according to the packaging is intended for safety purposes and ease of removal. That seems good. I would prefer not to have anything stuck inside me, you know?

Hunter smirks, grinning at me. "How's it feel?"

I want to point out that I'm the only one who's naked right now and I don't think I appreciate that. The least he could do is get naked with me. For, um... for moral support, you know?

...I have no idea how that makes sense but I just think it does...

"Um, it's okay?" I say, unsure what else to say. "I'm not sure it's--"

Hunter reaches out to help me up and off the bed so we can actually get dressed and not be late. I take his hand and pull with him, my body rising up, sitting, standing.

And, um...

Oh my gosh, what the heck.

The balls *move.* Um, inside me. *A lot.* It feels like a lot, at least. With every move I make, no matter what I'm doing, the balls shift and shuffle and roll inside me, which is an altogether strange but wonderful feeling. It's, um... it's really intense, actually.

Basically every time the balls move, my body clenches against them because, you know, I think it's just instinctive? I don't really know, but that's what happens. This makes the balls move *more,* which makes my... my pussy... clench down harder, and...

...Yup...

I wish I could say that's all I agreed to before we went to the Nightfall Cocktail Bar, but, nope, there's more.

The buzzing part? Uh huh...

PERFECTLY INNOCENT & COMPLETELY UNSUSPICIOUS

Episode 187

CHARLOTTE

After Hunter pulls me up off the bed while I'm still naked with my new ben wa balls inside me, um...

It takes me a second of accidental gasping to recognize the pattern. It's not like I'm going to have an instant O, I won't be going over the edge just from that, but, um... I'm pretty sure I *could* if I were doing the right thing? Like dancing, maybe? Or a brisk evening walk. Or... I don't know why but my mind immediately goes to pole dancing classes and I'm absolutely positive if I wore these during my amateur night performance I would've given everyone an entirely different kind of show.

"Fuck," Hunter grunts, biting his bottom lip, watching me struggle with the intense ecstasy clenching invisibly inside me. "You have no idea how hot that is."

"H-Hunter..." I whimper, trying to, um... to calm myself down...

It takes a second but if I stand really really still then, um... eventually the balls stop moving as much and it's mostly fine? Until I move again, and then it's decidedly not fine at all!

I'll get used to it. That's what I tell myself. It's fine. I'll get used to it. It's just intense right now because it's the first time I'm feeling this. It's, um... it won't be like this the entire time. Definitely not.

Oh, and in case this wasn't bad enough, I agreed to wear the vibrating panties and let Hunter control the remote. Which he reminds me of by taking said panties out of their package and helping me into them.

The panties themselves don't vibrate, but they have a small pocket in the front where this slim, curved vibrator fits. It curves perfectly against my kitty, the top nudging neatly and constantly against my pearl. It's actually not as bad as I thought it'd be. I can feel it, but it's more like a constant slight nudge and nothing too bad?

These are famous last words and I just don't want to think about them. How could I be so naive?!

Right, so, um... to top off my cocktail hour outfit, I wear this cute sundress I got with the cheerleaders and Jenny. I bought it online and it was really inexpensive and I love it so much but it's the first time I've ever worn it, so, um...

It's baby blue with tiny white polka dots. The thing I like most about it is the top covers everything. It buttons all the way up to my neck, and I guess I could unbutton some of the buttons but I like how it looks when it's buttoned up. It has a cute little collar like on a men's shirt but, um... you know, it's feminine? Then loose sleeves that go a quarter of the way down my arms. It's not a booby dress, which I like, because otherwise I think I'd be too embarrassed to wear it in public?

It's shorter than I would've preferred, but the skirt covers most of my thigh so it's fine. My lower thigh and knees aren't covered, but I think I can get used to that. It's, um... it's a work in progress and I put the dress on and do a twirl in the mirror, admiring my cute little outfit because I really want to look pretty for Hunter.

Twirling definitely does things inside me, though...

Hunter comes up behind me after we're dressed and he wraps his arms around me, hugging me tight. I lean back against him, smiling, excited. He kisses the side of my cheek, soft and sweet and lovely. I almost forget what I have going on down below, because I haven't moved much except for those little twirls to watch the skirt of my dress rise up slightly.

Hunter has the remote for my panties hidden in one hand and he pushes the button to turn them on as soon as he lulls me into soft sweet loveliness.

The vibrator pressing against my, um... I thought my clit would be most affected but honestly it's pretty strong and it feels good lower down, too. Oh, and the vibrations and my reaction send the balls inside me wild, so that's fun...

I gasp and my knees buckle slightly because I definitely wasn't expecting this. I don't fall because Hunter's holding me, but otherwise, um... yup...

My eyes roll into the back of my head as a clear path to ecstasy presents itself in the form of my vibrating panties and the ben wa balls.

Oh gosh I could definitely--

Hunter presses the button again, turning the vibrator off. My body buzzes for a couple seconds more, alive and ready, but then slowly and surely the pleasure fades to a light, persistent thrum.

"What do you think?" he asks as I stare wide-eyed into the mirror in front of us.

"Ummm... please d-don't do that too much..." I mumble.

"Shit, is it that good?"

"H-Hunter, I'm being *serious!*" I whine. "If... you do it and, um..."

"I *really* want to hear you say it out loud, Baby Sis," he says, smirking at me in the mirror.

"...I'll d-definitely have an *O* if you aren't careful..." I mutter.

My cheeks burn bright red and I'm tempted to do away with the plan altogether because I don't know if I can handle that level of embarrassment if, um... if I accidentally... like, in front of people?

Not that they'd *know,* but... I don't actually know if they'd know and now I'm imagining everyone somehow knowing and we get kicked out of the hotel for it and Francoise informs everyone we aren't even who we say we are, and the police come, and we're arrested for some obscure law I've never heard of but it's Las Vegas so who knows?

Then our parents have to come bail us out. In person. And they find out *everything.*

And that's how Hunter and I end up telling my mom and his dad we're, you know, um... *surprise!* We're dating...?

Please, no.

"I'll be good," Hunter says, smirking in a way that clearly indicates he may not actually be good.

"Okay..." I mumble, nodding along. "I, um... I *do* like it, b-but... baby steps, please?"

Hunter nods along. "Baby steps for Baby Sis. Got it."

"...It would be *really* fun if we were alone, though..." I add, because, yes. Yes it would.

"Yeah?" he asks, playing coy.

"*Mhm...*"

"Cool. Good to know. I'll keep it in mind for later..."

The doorbell to the Pomegranate Suite rings and it's Francoise and we have to leave, to go to cocktail hour for one long, torturous hour...

So, um, that's how that started. I don't know how it's going to end yet...

HUNTER

(Thirty minutes later, back in the Nightfall Cocktail Bar...)

When I get back from the bathroom, Baby Sis is hanging out with Francoise. She also looks flustered as hell. Holy fuck, it's kind of hot. I only realize she's holding a drink tightly in her hand when I join the two of them and Francoise promptly informs me she'll fetch me one, as well.

This gives me and my stepsister some alone time and we're pretending to be husband and wife for the weekend, so...

Look, we're supposed to schmooze or whatever the fuck they expect us to do here for an hour. I've never schmoozed in my entire life, though. I've gone to parties before, and those are cool and everything, but usually I chill with the boys and do whatever.

The guys aren't here. I'm with Baby Sis. I'm more than happy to chat it up with her and flirt like my life depends on it, especially considering what she has hidden under her sundress, but besides that--

Hold that thought for a second. Everything takes a backseat suddenly when Baby Sis glares at me with this vibrant, pleading look in her eyes, like she wants nothing more than for me to drag her somewhere private and completely fucking rock her world.

Which, you know, I'm down?

Except instead of suggesting that, she says, "Why did you *do* that?!"

And... no clue what she's talking about. Sorry?

"Do what exactly?" I ask.

"The remote," she says, sticking to as few words as possible. "You turned it on. When you were gone. It... it..." she stammers, trying to finish that thought, as if the mere memory is causing her issues. "It *buzzed!*" she says, finally squeaking it out.

"Oh," I say. Yeah, uh... "Shit, I didn't mean to do that."

She gives me this dubious as fuck look like she seriously doubts my sincerity right now. Damn, Baby Sis, calm down.

I don't say that, though. Even I know you're not supposed to say that shit to girls, especially when they look at you the way she's looking at me right now.

"You want to sit?" I offer, motioning to the fancy ass couch nearby. "Seriously, I was just randomly pushing buttons when I was in the bathroom. I didn't think it'd work from that far away. Maybe this was a bad--"

I'm about to accept the fact that we didn't think this through and we can cut it short with our fun and flirty toy game if she wants, but right as the words are nearly out of my mouth a couple things happen.

First, Francoise returns with my very own fancy blue-ish purple drink with silvery grey sparkles in it. Cool.

Second, before I can even take said drink off the silver platter in Francoise's hand, Baby Sis puts her own drink on the platter and says, "I, um... I need to go. To the bathroom. I... I w-won't be long!"

"Very well," Francoise says, a professional smile gracing her lips. "Mr. Jackson, please enjoy this non-alcoholic version of one of our mixologist's most popular drinks, the *Plus Ultra*. It's--"

She continues her spiel while I vaguely listen. Mostly because it's incredibly entertaining watching my stepsister try to maneuver her way through the room right now. Every quick step she takes sends the kegel balls into motion. I can see exactly what's happening by the look on her face and the way her eyes keep rolling into the back of her head every few steps.

To everyone else it probably just looks like she really has to use the bathroom?

Look, I feel kind of bad. Not entirely bad. But clearly this is an advanced sexual technique and she's a little out of her element at the moment.

Or so I think, but shortly after she disappears into the single stall bathroom down a short corridor, my phone buzzes.

I have a text message, ladies and gentlemen. It's from my stepsister.

BABY SIS

"Please turn the vibrating panties on and don't turn them off until I text you again and don't ask why and just don't okay bye."

I've never been more turned on in my life. Also, obviously I do exactly what she wants as quickly as humanly possible.

While taking a sip of my drink, acting casual, I shove my hand into my pocket, find the button to turn on the surprisingly strong vibrator in her sexy panties, and shove my thumb against it, hard, one single push.

Francoise stares at me as I sip my drink. I think she suspects something but clearly she doesn't know the scope of it. Please don't look down. I'm pretty sure the zipper of my pants is about to fucking break from how hard my cock is throbbing against it right now.

"Your thoughts?" she asks. "Is the drink to your liking?"

"Uh, yeah, it's good," I say, distracted. "It's got a nice, you know... thing to it..."

Francoise sighs and rolls her eyes. "A *thing* to it... yes, that's one way to explain a high-end luxury mocktail made with the finest ingredients. Of course."

A second later, my phone starts to ring. That was quick? Should I turn the vibrating panties off now?

Thankfully I don't, at least not yet, the reason for which will be obvious in, like, two fucking seconds.

"Sorry, important call!" I say, as if I do this all the time. "Business, you know? I need to take this. Be right back."

"*Business...*" Francoise drawls, shaking her head, rolling her eyes even harder. "Yes... of course..."

I step over to a private corner of the bar, slipping past other patrons who are way better at schmoozing than me.

Like I implied earlier, this literally takes all of two seconds and then I'm mostly by myself in a corner. I sit on the couch, answer the phone, a call from Baby Sis, presumably in the bathroom, also presumably to let me know I can turn her vibrating panties off now.

Except... nah...

I answer, holding the phone to my ear, and I'm immediately bombarded by her breathy, gasping moans. It takes me a second to realize she called me on accident.

"*Ohhhhhhhhhh,*" she whimpers, trying to keep it down so no one outside the bathroom hears her. "Yes! *Yes, please.* H-H-Hunter..."

If my cock wasn't already rock fucking hard, yeah, it's even harder than that now. What the fuck is harder than a rock? I mean, lots of stuff, but I'm struggling to think of anything at the moment.

Titanium. That's it. My cock is a rod of fucking titanium. There you go. I hope everyone's happy now.

I sit on the couch, trying not to choke on my *Plus Ultra* mocktail every time I take a sip, hoping no one sees me here and thinks it's an invitation to join me. I listen through the phone to my stepsister getting herself off in the bathroom, the rhythmic vibrations of her vibrating panties acting as a perfect backdrop to her lusty whimpers and moans of pleasure.

Her breath hitches, faster, harder. She gasps, squeaks, nearly squeals out in lust. Fuck, she's close. I listen to it all, imagining exactly what's going on as it happens. I nearly fucking bust a nut in my pants just from the sounds she's making, just from knowing what she's doing to herself.

Fuck...

This is how it goes in my head:

She's sitting on the closed lid of the toilet seat, surrounded by the marble walls of the bathroom with slate grey streaks running through the white stone like tiger stripes. Obviously she hiked her dress up for easy access to her pleasure, and she's leaning back against the wall, fingers pressed hard against the vibrator in her panties, guiding it to exactly where it needs to be. The kegel balls inside her are thrumming, her pussy clenching tight around them, trying to hold them in place except for the fact that it's literally impossible.

She moans, loud, gasping, panting, whimpering my name over and over as she gets closer and closer and so fucking close to her orgasm that I can taste it from here, through the phone, like a heady, intoxicating mix of cinnamon, spice, and everything sexy and nice.

To be fair that's probably from the mocktail in my hand. It really does have a lovely citrus flavor mixed with that Chinese five spice blend Francoise mentioned.

Look, yeah, anyways--

"*Please please please please!*" Baby Sis says, begging with some invisible force through the phone. Her breath catches, hitched, and suddenly she lets out a loud, ecstatic moan.

Frantic, in case anyone nearby can hear, I slam my thumb on my phone's volume button and turn that shit down. I can still hear her, though. I listen to every beautiful second as she gets herself off in the bathroom after I accidentally teased her a few minutes ago.

Holy fucking shit, I don't know if I can take this for much longer.

"*Oh!*" she squeaks after a second, giggling to herself, the vibrations probably overworking her clit.

She gets super sensitive after she has an *O* sometimes and needs a break. If I had to guess, this is one of those times.

Ignoring the bulge I can clearly feel when I put my hand in my pocket again, I push the off button on the remote. The vibration sound I could hear through the phone this whole time promptly cuts off. Baby Sis sounds confused at first, letting out a cute as fuck little noise, and then--

"...Oh no..." she says.

I don't know what that's for at first but suddenly she's talking to me over the phone so there you go.

"...Hello?" she says, hesitant.

"Yo," I say, the smirk in my voice as thick as an ice cream truck.

"...Ummmm, hi,"

"Having fun?" I ask.

"Please don't!" she squeaks.

"Look, not gonna lie, that was so fucking hot," I admit. "If you ever, I don't know, want to do it again sometime, I'm all for it."

"...Maybe!" she says, giggling. "I thought I accidentally called my mom, Hunter! How bad would that have been?"

"Pretty bad but also hilarious?"

"Shush!" she says. "It would *not* have been. I... I can't even... gosh."

"I don't want to rush you or anything but Francoise's staring at me. Maybe you should hurry back? I told her I had an important business call and I'm sitting in a corner right now hoping no one comes over."

"Oh," she says. "Um, okay. I'm, um... I'm going to take everything out, though? And off. I'm taking the balls out and I'm taking the, um... wait, I need panties. I'm n-not taking off my panties!" she informs me, as if I'd mind if she did.

Look, by all fucking means, Baby Sis...

"I'm taking the vibrator *out* of the panties..." she says, taking her time to get the words right. "And, um... c-can we play like that again later but maybe not when we have... you know, to go to a cocktail bar thing with Francoise?"

"Yes," I say, more sure about this than anything I've ever been sure about in my life. "Anytime you want. One-hundred percent. Abso-fucking-lutely."

"...Okay we don't have to if you really don't want to..." she says, hiding a flirty giggle in her voice.

"Dude."

"Dude!" she says, doing it right back to me.

"Get your sexy ass back here so I can grab it."

"Okay, be right out."

I do my best to ignore my raging hard erection as I stand up and head back to Francoise. I nod, as if this happens all the time, important business bullshit, you know the deal? Yeah yeah.

As soon as Baby Sis hurries back, no longer looking flustered, face glowing like a sexy goddess, I sneak a handful of her butt while she takes her drink back from Francoise.

Francoise gives us both a raised eyebrow look and sighs, letting out a quick tsk.

"You two," she says. "Be good."

CHARLOTTE

I feel a lot better after my, um... perfectly innocent and completely unsuspicious trip to the bathroom a little while ago...

I still can't believe I did that. Oh gosh. I especially can't believe I accidentally called Hunter *while* doing that, and then he stayed on the line, heard the entire thing, and--

Yes, so, I can't think about that right now because if I even so much as *start* to think about it my cheeks burn red and I remember the clinking balls and the small curved vibrator tucked into the handbag my mom let me borrow to bring to Las Vegas because I don't have one and it would probably be weird if I carried my book bag around the entire time, you know?

Right, um, anyways--

I have no idea what we're supposed to do during our hour in the Nightfall Cocktail Bar and apparently Hunter doesn't know, either?

"Look, no offense, I know this is your job, right?" Hunter

says, and I think he's being rhetorical but Francoise answers him.

"Yes, this is my job," she confirms. "Is everything to your satisfaction so far, Mr. Jackson?"

Hunter blinks, as if he didn't expect a question like that. I, um... now that she said it I think it makes perfect sense, but I didn't expect it, either.

"The mocktail's very good," I say, nodding. "Um, are there snacks, though?"

"Dude," Hunter says after I commandeer our butler for food purposes.

"The Nightfall is more of a stopover venue instead of a full service establishment," Francoise lets me know. "Unfortunately the only snacks I can arrange for you are a small assortment of mixed nuts and pretzels. Will that suffice, Ms. Scott?"

"Um, yes, please," I say. I haven't had pretzels in a long time and now I'm excited. "Thank you, Francoise!"

"Of course," she says with a curt, professional bow before heading to the bar to request said snacks from the bartender on duty.

Hunter keeps staring at me afterwards and I try to ignore it but it's hard. I also try to stare back at him but that's hard, too. He stares and I fidget and squirm and...

"Okay, look, pretzels and nuts sound pretty good," he finally says, reluctant to admit it. "But why are we even here?"

"...I don't know either," I say with a shrug. "Maybe ask Francoise when she gets back?"

"Dude!" Hunter says, duding me. "I was *going* to but then you asked her for snacks."

"Snacks are important!" I point out. "You said you wanted them, too. So, um, stop... d-don't look at me like that!"

Hunter keeps looking at me *exactly* like that except now it's kind of silly and flirty and I roll my eyes at him and sneak in for a quick kiss. He kisses me back and then takes my hand in his, holding it tight. I kind of like this whole pretend husband and wife thing, actually? It's fun and different.

Francoise's still negotiating with the bartender, who is apparently all out of nuts and pretzels? Or he's looking for them. I can't tell. It's a very heated conversation and Francoise seems determined to win, whatever there is to win, except the man behind the bar is trying to tell her it's impossible, no way, no how, not a chance, he's all out of--

Suddenly a man in a sparkling gold suit steps in front of us.

"Are you the ones?" he asks, sounding incredibly suspicious. "Dave and Barbara?"

And, um, okay so his entire suit isn't gold or sparkling. It's kind of black, at least as a background. His suit is like a painting and the backdrop is velvety black but then over that, inlaid like the intricate designs you'd likely see on ancient architecture, is an assortment of detailed gold leaf designs that sparkle and shine in the cool blue lighting of the Nightfall Cocktail Bar.

"...Are we supposed to know you?" Hunter asks, possibly also sounding incredibly suspicious.

"Ha!" the man says, laughing loud. "Are *you* supposed to know *me*? Sir, please. I'm *the* guy to know around here. If you know me, you know *everyone.* Trust me."

"I... I don't know you and I don't really know everyone else, either?" I point out, unsure if I should be admitting this.

The man in the golden suit blinks and looks at me. I have no idea why or what he's thinking.

Right then Francoise returns, smiling wide, carrying a small silver platter with a porcelain bowl on top. It's double-sided, half the bowl sectioned off for pretzels while the other half contains an assortment of mixed nuts. She triumphantly displays her prize before us like it's a treasured catch she made during an especially strenuous hunt in the deep jungle.

The gold suited man helps himself to one of my pretzels, popping it in his mouth and chewing.

"Oh, I know Francoise, though," I say, just now remembering I *do* know someone here even if it's not exactly everyone.

"Mr. Jackson and Ms. Scott," Francoise says, nodding politely to us before introducing the man. "This is the general manager of the Metropolitan Signature hotel. He's the reason you're here today."

Oh no...

Would my mom and Hunter's dad know that? Did we screw up? Are we about to get kicked out now?

Seriously, pretending to be my mom is way harder than I thought it'd be and I didn't even think it'd be easy in the first place.

"The name's Anthony," he says, holding his hand out to Hunter. Hunter shakes it and Anthony lifts one brow, playfully acknowledging Hunter's firm grip, before letting loose and doing the same to me. I, um... I shake his hand but I don't think I'm as grippy as Hunter because I don't get a brow lift.

"This is a nice hotel you have here?" Hunter says, attempting to schmooze.

"*Nice?*" Anthony says, sighing and shaking his head. "Sir. This is *the* establishment to frequent when you're in Vegas. Which is why you're here. Listen, I know why you're actually here. You won the slot machine jackpot prize, yeah? But now that you've had a taste of what we offer, and, trust me, there's more where that came from, this is going to be *the* place you come to when you're in Vegas from now on. You know why that is?"

"Is it the pretzels?" I ask, because he reaches for another, popping it in his mouth while waiting for us to answer.

Francoise's lips curl up into a smooth grin and it looks like she's trying not to laugh. She's a lot better at it than I would be. She doesn't even break.

Anthony takes a moment to chew and swallow and then says, "These? Nah. Look, I'm not supposed to tell you this, but they're from Costco. Nothing fancy. You can grab a massive bag anytime you want. Do you have a membership?"

"No," Hunter says, shaking his head.

"My mom does," I say without thinking.

"Your mother's a smart woman!" Anthony says with a blackjack dealer's grin. "Anyways, I invited you here personally. Yes, it was me. Personally. Francoise made it happen. She's great, isn't she? Anyways, enough about Francoise. She's a little too great if you know what I mean? We'd be talking about her all day if I had to tell you all the great things about her. So here. Take these. This, too. On the house. Part of the prize package. Enjoy the show and don't spend the free play all in one place, my friends."

Anthony hands me a plastic card and Hunter a pair of shiny paper tickets. I take the card and hold it in both hands in front of me because I don't know what else to do with it. Hunter blinks and glances down, reading the tickets.

"Please note that you actually do need to spend the free play all in one place as it's only valid in our casino," Francoise says, giving us a personal disclaimer.

"See?" Anthony says, laughing boisterously. "She's great! Knows everything. What'd I tell ya? Anyways, thanks for coming down. We're about to wind this shindig up. Did you have a cocktail? The *Plus Ultra* is fantastic. You got them one, right? Tell me you didn't leave our VIPs hanging, Francoise?"

"Mr. Jackson and Ms. Scott have been well taken care of," Francoise informs him with a curt nod. "No need to worry, sir."

"See? See?" he says, motioning towards her. "Let me know if you need anything else. And enjoy dinner! It's great.

Everything here is, but dinner's really great. You're gonna love it."

With that, Anthony strolls off, his gold decorated suit flashing and sparkling with each step he takes. He kind of looks like a walking disco ball but just gold and somehow it works really well.

"It's twenty dollars worth of free play in the casino and tickets to a local burlesque show," Francoise explains. "While your attendance isn't mandatory, I highly recommend the entertainment. I know many of the performers and they're all--"

"Holy fucking shit," Hunter says, holding the tickets up like we just won the ultra mega grand prize jackpot at a casino that consists of a luxury weekend getaway in a high-end hotel *and* a puppy. "Dude, Baby Sis, check this shit out."

"H-Hunter!" I squeak. "I'm, um... B-Barbara... shhhhhh!"

"Yeah yeah, whatever," he grunts before shoving the tickets at me.

It takes me a second to understand what I'm reading because the font looks like it belongs on the title screen of a horror movie and not for a scandalous burlesque show, but, um...

"...Huh?" I mumble, confused. "Really?"

"Yes," Francoise says, as if fully understanding where my confusion lies.

...We're now the proud owners of tickets to go see the Zombie Burlesque show and I really don't know how I feel about that...

"I don't want to say this is the most amazing thing that's ever happened to me because, let's be real, a lot of amazing shit happens to me sometimes. Like that business phone call earlier, which was definitely for business purposes. Absolutely amazing. Uh, right, anyways, this is one of the most amazing things to happen to me in, like... a couple of minutes, and I'm ready for it."

That's Hunter, who is now very excited to go see dancing zombies.

"Do the zombies get naked, though?" I ask. "Why do we want to see naked zombies?"

"You're seriously overthinking this," Hunter says.

"The zombies *do* in fact remove certain articles of clothes, but in a tasteful and, dare I say, classy manner?" Francoise informs us. "It's quite impressive."

"Fuck yeah it is," Hunter says, still very much excited.

"Um, okay," I mumble. "Is it just girls? Girl zombies?"

"There's men, as well," Francoise says. "They're very progressive zombies."

"Who even cares?" Hunter says. "Fuck, man... zombies..."

"I take it you'll be partaking of that particular piece of entertainment tomorrow night, then?" Francoise asks.

"I guess so?" I say.

"Yes," Hunter says, much more definitive.

As for tonight, though?

———

Can't get enough of Hunter and Charlotte's story?
Keep reading right away!
Stepbrother, Please Stop Teasing Me! (Volume Fifteen)

A NOTE FROM MIA

Make sure you don't miss any of my new releases by signing up for my VIP readers list!
Cherrylily.com/Mia

Hi!

We're heading to Vegas, baby!

First off, I hope you loved the end of the Stepbrother Triathlon challenges. I thought the stripclub episodes were super fun, but I did want to make sure to finish everything off definitively so I had the idea of doing the Final Exam right after, haha.

I thought it'd be hilarious to have Charlotte's take versus Erica's, and portray it in the most straightforward way possible with each of them answering some wild and insane questions that Erica came up with.

And then, you know, we're heading into summer break! Those episodes are going to be a ton of fun with a lot going on, and maybe some new hookups on the horizon? We're only just brushing the surface as far as Teddy and Angela go, but also, hm, more Hannah and Olly?

We've also had a longstanding, on again off again, sometimes fighting, sometimes loving, interesting situation between Clarissa and her mysterious stepbrother that will pop up again too, so...

Who exactly is he and will Clarissa find love or lust with him again this summer? Hmm.

For now, we're heading into the Vegas Getaway episodes and I think they started out strong in this one. I have more to come and they set the scene for a lot of what happens in the future.

Also, I just really wanted to give Hunter and Charlotte some alone time since I think they deserve it, you know? This was a good excuse for me to write some nice steamy scenes, too. Haha. I think the ben wa balls predicament is one of my favorites they've been through together, but there's more coming up later on, too.

I wonder how the weekend will go, though?

Is it true that what happens in Vegas stays in Vegas? I guess that depends on what actually happens...

You'll find out in the next volume, and then we're heading into some summer break fun immediately afterwards! I really love the summer break episodes since they have a different feel to them. A lot can happen during summer break, right?

If you're enjoying Hunter and Charlotte's story, I'd love love love if you could leave a review! Reviews are kind of like giving an author a bonus tip, like at a restaurant, and I really appreciate them so much.

What do you think of the start of summer with the girls shopping trip plan? And how about Charlotte finally finishing her first romance novel? She got the steamy scenes in and everything! What do you think of the start of their weekend in Vegas and where do you think it'll go from here?

A NOTE FROM MIA

Thanks so much for reading Stepbrother, Please Stop Teasing Me! I can't wait to show you how Hunter and Charlotte's summer goes!

~**Mia** ^_^

ABOUT THE AUTHOR

Mia loves to have fun in all aspects of her life. Whether she's out enjoying the beautiful weather or spending time at home reading a book, a smile is never far from her face. She's prone to random bouts of laughter at nothing in particular except for whatever idea amuses her at any given moment.

Sometimes you just need to enjoy life, right?

She loves to read, dance, cuddle with her cat, and explore outdoors. Coffee and bubble baths are two of her favorite things. Flowers are especially nice, and she could get lost in a garden if it's big enough and no one's around to remind her that there are other things to do.

She comes from New England, where the weather is beautiful and the autumn colors are amazing.

You can find the rest of her books (here) or email her any time at mia@cherrylily.com if you have questions, comments, or if you just want to say hi!

ALSO BY MIA CLARK

Stepbrother With Benefits 1

"Friends with benefits, stepbrother with benefits, what's the difference?"

"Um, we're not even friends, Ethan?"

Rule #1 - It's only supposed to last for a week…

Daddy Issues

Good girls get cuddled. Bad girls get spanked…

Keep it up and you're mine, Fiona. Forever.

A Thousand Second Chances 1

Gavin Knight has a secret he can't tell anyone…

He's reliving the same day over and over again.

Trapped in a time loop? Might as well be a bad boy, right?

It's going great up until he meets Everly Adams, the only girl who's stuck in the same situation, and remembers *everything*…

Milton Keynes UK
Ingram Content Group UK Ltd.
UKHW051048021223
433483UK00021B/1167